Hearts in a Labyrinth

Table of Contents

About the Author

June A. Ramsay enjoys crafting passionate, faith-based stories that focus on characters who face victimization—some caused by the cruelty of others, life's inequalities, and family discord. She showcases how one can rise above unimaginable situations by paying attention and following the still, small voice within. That voice that knows everything.

June's interests expanded to include gardening and interior decorating. She is very creative and says her imagination developed during her childhood, which was spent without television.

Born in British Guiana (now Guyana), June grew up in a Christian community. After migrating to the USA as a young adult, she built a career in executive business administration, working for the 'Big 5 Accounting Firms' while returning to college and earning an interdisciplinary bachelor's degree from Empire State College, New York.

Author's Website: Juneramsay.com

Works by the author:

Books

I Said, "I Am A Nun"

By The Riverside

Her Father's Sin

Journals

International Women's Day

Forgiveness Journal

Write It Down, So You Remember!

SHORT STORY 1

When Life Falls Apart

Does It Fall Into Place?

"Sometimes good things fall apart so better things can fall together."

~ Marilyn Monroe

Introduction

This short story, 'When Life Falls Apart,' is a compilation of thoughts and ideas about picking up the pieces of your life when it falls apart because, at some point, if you live long enough, it will.

We make many plans throughout life—plans we believe are rock-solid. Then we follow them with confidence to bring them to fruition.

Imagine a wedding—a woman marrying the man she believes is meant to be her husband, the man of her dreams, with the expectation of spending the rest of her life with him in marital bliss. This was her decision, not one in which God was consulted. She dated him, he said things that made her feel special, promised her forever love, stirred her emotions, and before too long, she was in love and getting married. In time, this marriage may fall apart beyond repair. The main reason is that God was not consulted, and He was not in it. This was a situation where the woman was doing things on her own.

Many of us do this, whether it's getting married, getting a job, buying a home, or moving to a different place.

We need to stop feeling good and making plans without consulting God to see what He has planned for us. So, let's stop feeling good and start feeling God.

Author's Note

I was inspired to write this short story after watching a video about a young man who ran from a tiger to save his life. As he ran, he saw a well and jumped into it. At the bottom of the well was a cobra waiting to devour him. He clung to a branch that kept him suspended between the tiger above and the cobra below. While he was wondering what to do next, a rodent appeared and began chewing on the branch he was holding on to for dear life.

The tiger, growing impatient, decided to jump into the well to reach the young man. As it leaped, it landed on top of the cobra, breaking its neck. Both the tiger and the cobra died instantly.

The young man climbed out of the well and continued on his journey.

At one point in his devastating predicament, he had felt hopeless and trapped with a tiger over his head, a cobra at his feet, and a rodent steadily gnawing away at his only lifeline. He saw no way out. His life seemed to be falling apart. Yet, when the tiger jumped into the well and killed the cobra, the entire situation changed. The danger was gone, and his path was clear.

Sometimes life appears impossible, with no way forward, but there is always a way out.

That video inspired me to write this short story while weaving in some of my own life experiences about times when

everything seemed to fall apart, only to fall into place eventually. I have also included some personal strategies I use to keep myself grounded during life's challenges. When life seems to be unraveling, I remind myself to shift perspective and change the scenario.

I hope you enjoy this short story and the suggestions I have shared.

You can reach me directly at <u>Juneology1@yahoo.com</u>. Or through my website **Juneramsay.com**, where you can also purchase my books and journals.

My best to you,

JRam

When Life Falls Apart

- Does it fall into place?

Imagine this: The plan was fantastic. Everything was on schedule. Everything looked right. Then, before you know it, the bottom of the plan fell out. How could this be?

Have you ever felt this way? Have you ever had an excellent plan that you poured all of yourself, energy, time, and resources into, only to have it fall apart beyond repair? It is like a beautiful glass vase falling on a ceramic-tiled floor, shattering all its beauty into tiny pieces that can never be restored.

What do you do? The vase cannot be repaired. It's like a death, and dead things must be tossed out or buried. Then, after you bury it, you must grieve the loss, leave the place of burial, and move on, whether you want to or not. There is no other way.

I will refer to people, places, and things as "Noun Factors," because all our "falling apart" issues involve a person, a place, or a thing.

Let's think about these statements:

- *The promise of forever.*

- *He promised to love you until death do you part, but he changed his mind after the fundamental issues of daily life overpowered him.*

- *He found someone else whom he wants to invest his time and energy.*
- *He had extramarital affairs and hid them from you, but when you found out, everything fell apart.*
- *You lost your dream job.*
- *You were betrayed.*
- *Someone you love passed away.*
- *You lost on a deal.*
- *The stock market crashed.*
- *You fell ill.*
- *You were accused of doing something you did not do.*
- *You had something better than another person, and they hated you for it.*
- *People you trusted stole from you because they felt you did not deserve what you had, the very things you worked and sacrificed for. They believed they needed it, so they took it.*

Suppose you have experienced any of these situations or anything similar. If you have, you might find some comfort in this "short" story about life after loss, life after betrayal, picking up the pieces, and starting over.

Let us take a look at how life can fall into place after it falls apart.

Whether you are dealing with a current "falling apart" situation or have faced one in the past, here are some thoughts and ideas to ponder, with the hope that they keep you grounded. Or, if you have never had a plan that fell apart, it

might still be helpful to read this as preparation for the future—or to share and comfort a loved one going through their falling-apart scenario.

As you can see from the limited list of scenarios I mentioned, life can fall apart for many different reasons and at various crossroads, leaving you lost and hopeless. It often falls apart because of deceit, jealousy, covetousness, trust issues, broken promises, and death.

When life falls apart, it leaves dreams and relationships shattered. People split up and fight over the very things they once accumulated in love. Sometimes, they would rather destroy an item of value than see a former loved one have it.

Things falling apart often result in heartache, hurt, and rarely a win-win outcome. In some cases, there is even physical injury and, sadly, sometimes murder.

These situations are irretrievable. Yet, over time, depending on the circumstances, there can be healing as the pain lessens, and in that healing, life can fall back into place.

It seems inevitable that life must fall apart at certain stages and under specific circumstances, allowing things to fall into their rightful place. Life falls apart to help you see things clearly and understand what you are doing and who you are with. I believe that life often falls apart when it is not pleasing to God, allowing for clarity on how to move forward.

Nonetheless, there are lessons to be learned in every "falling apart" disappointment. I think life must fall apart at times so it can fall into its proper place.

When we look back on our lives over specific periods, such as months, years, or even decades, we often find ourselves thankful for the "Noun Factor" that brought our lives into disarray. I hear people say all the time, including myself, "I am so glad I am not with, or in that 'Noun Factor' situation." Thank God things worked out the way they did, despite the pain, because if that hadn't happened, we might not have the opportunities we have now or be where we are today.

Recently, I heard someone say, "You need to send flowers to the people who walked away from you, disappointed you, stole from you, betrayed you, and so on, along with a thank-you card." I thought to myself, that's a fantastic idea… I need to buy a lot of flowers and a great selection of beautiful thank-you cards to send to all the people in my life who deserve praise and thanks for disappointing me, for being envious toward me, stealing from me, or being part of unfair job situations, stock market losses, and so forth. To all those "Noun Factor" situations—Thank you!

As I write this narrative, I find myself wondering: Did my life fall into place after it fell apart? The answer is a resounding "Yes." It fell into place each time I was let down and disappointed. I am genuinely thankful for all the 'Noun Factors' of my life. If those events had not occurred and changed the trajectory of my life, I might not be as happy as I am now. My life has fallen into a place I love and appreciate. I am loving my life. From all those falling-apart situations, I now have an overflowing joy. Why? Because each time I was let down, I went to God, and He mended my broken heart.

"He heals the brokenhearted and binds up their wounds."

~Psalm 147:3

Under no circumstances would I want to be back in any situation with any "Noun Factor" from my past.

We must understand that no one can do anything to us without God's permission. If He allows it, then He has a plan to bless us, to teach us, and to bring us out of it so that we know who healed us and who set our feet back on solid ground. Our focus must remain on Him. When people intentionally cause us to rearrange our lives, change direction, and re-evaluate what we are doing and why, it is often because we were not on God's plan.

We must know with certainty that the essence of who we are is that God is in us. So, when we are rejected, perhaps simply for being ourselves, it is a rejection of God in us. We are all God's children, created by Him to be who He wants us to be and to do what He has placed us here to do. No one has the right to expect us to become what they think we should be for their gain.

Having a Plan

– Something to fall back on

Do you have a plan for your life? If the "Genie" jumped out of the bottle and asked you, "What are your three wishes?" Would you know what they are? Do you have a plan, or are

you simply drifting through life, accepting whatever comes your way?

I am a planner. I like to plan the things I want to see manifest in my life. This gives me clear direction on what I need to work toward. What I know for sure is that without a plan for my life, I risk following someone else's, which may not have my best interests at heart. Often, the plan was designed to benefit them, not me. I speak collectively here: if you do not have a plan for yourself, be cautious of those who try to pull you into theirs.

Having a plan means you are using the brain God gave you to create and advance your own desires. We are all designed with innate desires. So, it does not mean you are not listening to God and following His plan; it means you are documenting what you would like to see in your life, and with every plan, you must submit to God for guidance and execution, because we can do nothing on our own.

Many years ago, when I was beginning my career, I was asked in an interview, "Where do you see yourself in five years?" The question was intended to focus on my job, but after I answered it, I turned it into a personal life-planning question.

I started outlining what I wanted to achieve and where I envisioned myself in five, ten, fifteen, twenty years, and beyond. I became specific about my goals, breaking them down into yearly, monthly, and weekly steps. Each day, as I sat at my desk, I wrote down what I wanted to achieve that day,

taking small, deliberate steps toward bigger goals. I always remind myself: *the longest journey begins with the first step.* And regularly checking in with myself helps keep me focused.

Every year, I set goals, write them down, and assign timelines. I always have something lined up to work on, which I call my "What Ifs: Plan A, Plan B, and Plan C". This approach means that no one can honestly divert me from my path; they might only push me to the next plan. If Plan A fails, I analyze the situation, close that chapter, grieve the loss, and shift my focus to Plan B. At that point, Plan B becomes the new Plan A. I never live without these three plans. I always have a "What If" plan, just in case. Because you never know if or when life may fall apart.

Living this way has taught me to be flexible. Life will throw curveballs, and you have to bend with them; rigidity does not work well. Another important principle for me is living detached from the "Noun Factors:" people, places, and things. It's beneficial to practice detachment because one day you may find yourself detached from what you feel you need to cling to, and often it won't be by choice.

For example, when your time on this planet ends, you will leave everything and everyone behind. We come with nothing, become attached to everything, and then go with nothing.

When we truly accept that we arrive in this world with nothing and will leave with nothing, it becomes an empowering realization. We all know this in theory, but once we internalize it, we stop fighting over material possessions

and things that don't belong to us. We handle situations in a way that preserves our peace of mind. Peace comes from God and should not be disturbed by anyone.

This way of thinking allows me to give fully of myself and my resources in whatever I do. I never work halfway; I give my all. If it doesn't work out, I can walk away with a clear conscience. I believe in doing my best and then letting the outcome unfold as it may. If things don't work out, I know I did my best and am free to move on.

Living this way has given me a strong sense of direction. Having a plan provides both guidance and purpose. It also means I am rarely surprised or devastated by anyone's actions for long. I may be caught off guard at first, but not for long.

Each month, I review my progress toward my goals. Sometimes the progress is small, but even small steps bring me joy. They are bite-sized pieces of my dreams being added to the pile of completion. After reviewing, I focus on the new month, project what I want to achieve, and write it down. At the bottom of everything I write down that I desire, and I close it by writing the following:

'These or better things now manifest for me in totally harmonious and peaceful ways for the highest good of all concerned, in Jesus Christ's mighty name. Amen.'

I did not create that statement, and I am not sure who shared it with me, but I use it constantly.

I treat each approaching new month in the same way we do at the end of the year. As we start a New Year, there are

always resolutions and things we want to do and achieve. So, I set my goals, outlining what I would like to happen that year.

Often, I jot down ideas on loose pieces of paper or in my journals, only to forget about them. Then later, while thumbing through old notes, I'm often surprised and in awe of how much I've accomplished that I had once written down. I believe there is a kind of magic in putting ink to paper.

For example, throughout history, everything necessary has been recorded: the Bible as a guide for living, every law, the Constitution, and all agreements. If you have a Will for your life, it has to be written down. Plans for companies are written down, among other things.

My love for writing and journaling inspired me to create my collection of journals, which I publish on my website under *June's Journals* at **juneramsay.com**. The motto for my journals is:

"Write it down so you don't forget, and it may manifest."

When you write things down, you tell the universe, "I am in the game, and I want to participate." As I navigate this game of life, when situations start to unravel, I step back, observe how they disintegrate, and let them fall apart. I do not cling to what is leaving me, because if my destiny is tied to it, it cannot go, and if it's mine, I cannot lose it.

What If Everything Happens for a Reason?

My late maternal grandmother often said, "Everything happens for the best." As a child, I couldn't comprehend her statement, and I often wondered about it in my young mind. But as I have matured, I now understand what she meant: do not try to bend the hand of fate. There are natural laws that govern our lives, whether we are aware of them or not, and those laws work behind the scenes, pulling their strings as the universe dictates, under the direction of the Almighty Father.

"The earth is the LORD's, and the fullness thereof; the world, and they that dwell therein."

~ Psalms 24:1–2

Examining my life, the lives of those I have had the privilege to know, and even the world in general, I have concluded that life often falls into place only after it falls apart. Sometimes our lives are in disarray, and uphill battles arise when we insist on doing things our way —the wrong way. Often, following what I call the "Noun Factor," life must fall apart before it can fall into its rightful place. It's like putting together a puzzle and forcing pieces into spots where they do not belong, only to reach the end and realize you must dismantle it and start over. Just as each puzzle piece must be placed where it is designed to fit, our lives also have specific destinations that are meant to be fulfilled. When we are not

headed in the right direction, life will reconfigure our path to get us back on track.

When driving with a GPS, I often laugh at myself for ignoring the given directions. I turn where I want to, not where I am instructed, and then the system recalibrates. That simple message, "Recalculating," serves as a small reminder that life, too, can recalibrate, moving us away from wrong situations and circumstances.

I believe that when things fall apart, it is an opportunity to correct certain aspects of our lives, examine what we are doing and why, and then recalibrate, choosing God's direction as the right path.

How do you know what God's direction is? We must ask for guidance and listen for the answer. We must pay attention to what you genuinely desire and explore it. Consider whether your thoughts and desires are Godly. For instance, would the most important people in your life approve of the thoughts you are entertaining? For example, if you are considering a relationship with someone you know is not right for you—you are not equally yoked, but you follow your flesh because it feels good—that is not good. If you are not equally yoked, that isn't good either. Would you feel comfortable sharing this with your mother or your closest confidants? If not, something is wrong. Recalibrate.

In the end, we must place the pieces of our lives in their proper places so the whole picture appears as it was meant to

be. Sometimes that means dismantling what we have built and rebuilding it the right way, God's way.

Life cannot fall into place if we knowingly make wrong decisions —simply because they feel good, because we believe we know better, or because we assume this "Noun Factor" is meant for us. We must ask ourselves: What does the Bible say about this? Sadly, many of us continue in the wrong for a long time until the rug is pulled out from under us or we are forced to face judgment. Yes, God is forgiving, but forgiveness requires repentance: we must turn away from wrongdoing, seek His forgiveness, and stop repeating the same actions.

In the Bible, there are examples of people being forgiven and then instructed to sin no more. There comes a point when doing what feels good should no longer be our guide; we must choose what is right.

Too often, we persist in doing wrong because it pleases the heart. However, remember that the heart can be deceitful. Sometimes we are forced to move forward without the "Noun Factor," which can lead to significant losses, pain, and sadness. Yet, in that breaking apart, life falls into the right place —a better place we could not have imagined without the loss.

Looking back, you will understand, just as the Apostle Paul said,

"I have learned, in whatsoever state I am, therewith to be content."

~ Philippians 4:11

We should also give God praise and thanks when things fall apart, because we know He is doing a better work in us and for us through that very process.

In every situation, we must seek to understand what happened, so we can learn from it and avoid falling into the same disarray again. If we do not learn from our mistakes, we are bound to repeat them.

Every "Noun Factor" can be placed into one of three categories: a reason, a season, or a lifetime. Some "Noun Factors" are for a reason, some for a season, and some for a lifetime. When the reason ends, let it go. When the season is over, move on. And when it's for a lifetime, it will simply be. It will remain with you for the rest of your life. You do not need to fight for what is genuinely yours, nor cling to what belongs to someone else. What is meant for you will come to you in its time.

Life is short. Avoid building something permanent in a temporary situation.

"When people show you who they are, believe them."

~ Maya Angelou

When we sincerely seek the divine plan for our lives, we stop telling God what to do and calling it prayer. We stop

asking Him to bless the mess we create. I have even seen slogans saying, *"God, please bless this mess."* Looking back on my own life, I recall praying for specific things when, in truth, I was trying to bend God's hand, telling Him what I wanted and asking Him to bless it, rather than asking Him to reveal His divine plan for me. But, my goodness, did I learn.

What Constitutes Life Falling Apart?

Life falls apart for many reasons: a breakup, divorce, job loss, financial ruin, betrayal, illness, or death. When we face any of these situations, it can feel like the end of the world. We ask ourselves, *Why me? What am I to do now? I cannot handle this. How could the "Noun Factor" do this to me, or take this from me?*

Remember, life happens, that's why. Life is a constant rotation of situations, day after day. People change their minds. They get better offers. They believe something better awaits them. They may feel they did not receive enough from you, and you did not do enough for them. Companies decide they can get better work for less pay. These are life's challenges. So, the question is not *why* this happens to you, but *when* it will happen. If you live long enough, you will experience some part of your life unexpectedly falling apart.

When it does—and it will—seek Godly ways to handle it.

God will always show you the right path. This may mean walking away from the "Noun Factor," cutting your losses, and moving on. It may mean leaving a familiar area and

embarking on a new chapter in an unfamiliar place. There is something truly remarkable about a "New Start." Let the "Noun Factors" fade from your life, along with everything connected to them and the memories they carry.

Personally, during some of my life challenges, I couldn't stay in the place where the misery was poured onto me, so I moved. This resulted in my learning a new city or town, and sometimes in a completely different state. In the process of moving and recalibrating, I grew, learn, and came to understand myself better.

This is a vast, abundant universe with more than enough for every one of us. There is no need to cling to any "Noun Factor" – adhere to God and His directions.

Burn, Burry, or Flush

I will get personal here and share some of the things I have done throughout my many disappointments. First, I do what we all do, what is natural… I go through the initial shock and disbelief, then I have my pity party for as long as I need. An invitation may be extended to one or two guests whom I know will help me see the whole picture clearly and in a Godly way while also comforting me.

When the pity party is over, I start journaling, either in my physical paper journal or on my computer. Whichever method I choose, it always leads to pages and pages of my feelings pouring out. Through this, I release the hurt and disappointment that I have experienced.

Sometimes I write a letter to the "Noun Factor" that caused the anguish. In these letters, I pour out my soul, my anger, my hurt, my disappointment, and my expectation of better, as well as how I lost my trust in the person. These letters are never mailed. When typing an email, I avoid putting any names in the recipient box, just in case I accidentally hit send. I title the subject line with the topic that's bothering me, then I let my feelings flow. This process could take days or weeks, depending on the depth of the disappointment.

When I feel I have exhausted all my resources, I print the document. If it's journal pages, I tear them out of the journal and keep them for a while—no particular length of time. I may even place them in my Bible. Then, when I feel entirely ready, I dispose of the pages in one of the following ways:

- **I burn the pages.** *I keep a huge aluminum mixing bowl that one of my sisters gave me. I find it perfect for burning these pages because it is broad and deep, fitting right under the faucet in my kitchen sink. After the burning is complete, I put the ashes in my garden bed or a plant pot to nourish my plants, as ashes are beneficial to the soil.*

- **I bury the pages.** *I tear them into shreds and bury them in my garden, where they eventually decompose into compost, which is always beneficial to the soil.*

- **I flush the pages.** *On some occasions, depending on how I feel, I soak the pages in water and then flush them down the toilet to make disposal easier.*

As I burn, bury, or flush the pages, I say a releasing affirmation, such as:

Dear "___,"

In the name of the Almighty Father of heaven and earth, I forgive you, I bless you, I release you, and I set you free. Your thoughts, words, and actions have no power over me, now and forever.

Amen.

If I need more affirmations, I adapt the wording from this one and add whatever else feels right for the situation. I continue using these affirmations for as long as necessary.

Get Rid of Reminders

Just like after a divorce, you take the wedding ring off. The marriage is over, and the ring represented that commitment, so let it go. Why would you keep wearing it? This principle is not limited to weddings and divorces; it applies to any relationship or friendship, regardless of its nature. Why would you hold on to something from someone you may now resent? Ecclesiastes reminds us that there is a time for everything under the Sun – a time to love and a time to hate, especially if you were the one hurt.

Why would you want to keep anything that reminds you of that "Noun Factor?" Do you think such an item will bring you blessings now? No, it will not. These things become accursed

items because the energy of that "Noun Factor" is infused in them. Do you really want those things around you?

After any disappointment, I go through my space and remove anything that person gave me. If I find valuable gold jewelry, I either have it remade into something different, give it away, or sell it. You must release the energy those objects hold. Sometimes I burn items in my backyard fire drum. Other items are trashed, and those in good condition are given to Goodwill. I do not allow those energies to linger around me. Because at that point, I am starting fresh and clear, without the old "Noun Factors" in my life.

In the case of a divorce, it's a good idea to clear out anything that reminds you of the marriage—gifts, jewelry, and so on. This is a good time to give away or transform belongings. I even recommend moving out of the shared residence if possible. If that's not an option, repainting the interior with a new color and removing as much furniture as possible can help. Even if finances are tight, this is a good time to use your credit responsibly, as there's a deep satisfaction in buying new things and redoing an old space.

You can't start a new life surrounded by old things, old memories, and old stagnant energy.

Many say you should not keep or use old towels, sheets, clothing, sleepwear, lingerie, coats, handbags, or similar items from someone you are now separated from. Only retain valuable jewelry that can be remade, exchanged, or sold.

Remember: when something is dead, bury it. When something ends, move on. Even your dearest loved ones must be left at the cemetery after death. There can be no resurrection without a burial, and you must resurrect from the situation. You must undergo the burial of what no longer serves you to rise to new circumstances and a new way of life.

If you are dealing with a job loss, let it go. Never mourn a job, regardless of position, pay, colleagues, or benefits. When a job ends, it means your destiny was not tied to that position. Maintain relationships with valuable people you met there, but move forward. Remember, this universe is abundant, and something better awaits you.

We must remember that every disappointment carries seeds of opportunity and new benefits. When things fall apart, there is freedom from the stress and negativity of the situation and the "Noun Factors" involved. You gain the freedom to create favorable new circumstances.

It is difficult when life falls apart, but by leaning on God and taking time for activities you enjoy that are God-approved —such as reading stories from the Bible and looking at what some people endured, or simple pleasures like eating ice cream or whatever you like —you will heal day by day, moving past the "Noun Factors."

Another helpful practice is to find Bible verses relevant to your situation and read them repeatedly. I find many encouraging passages in the Psalms, although inspiration is evident throughout the Bible. Writing verses on a wall, mirror,

or dashboard —somewhere you see often —reinforces their message.

After completing these steps, focus on yourself. Forgive the entire situation, let it go… then forgive yourself. I use a "Forgiveness Journal" with prompts to guide the process. Be kind to yourself.

Some situations take longer to overcome than others, depending on their severity. Be patient with yourself and avoid rushing. Reflect on activities that bring you joy, such as old hobbies, and bring them back into your life. Take care of yourself by cooking meals you enjoy, finding and using delicious recipes, reading your favorite books, or revisiting old ones. Listen to music you love, rewatch your favorite movies, and nurture your enjoyment of life. Reclaim your freedom and never take it for granted.

I have never encountered a situation where life fell apart and did not eventually fall into place. Looking back, I am grateful for everything that did not work out for me. I often say that God shook me to redirect me when I was headed the wrong way.

Many people have said that when things fell apart and caused losses — such as losing wealth, health, or freedom — it turned out to be the best thing that happened to them. Loss often teaches us to appreciate a new normal.

After a fire, for example, some have said the event was beneficial because insurance allowed them to rebuild a better

home, thereby avoiding the complications of repairing the former house.

Whatever the situation, self-care and self-love are paramount. No one loves you more than God.

Remember, you are whole as you are, without those "Noun Factors." So, return to your wholeness.

Now, reflect on your own life struggles. Consider a time when your life fell apart and ask yourself:

"When my life fell apart, did it fall into place?"

The End

SHORT STORY 2

The Voice of My Soul

The Voice of My Soul

Many who weren't born into wealth had to figure out how to earn a living while simultaneously pursuing their dreams.

In an effort to make ends meet, they took on jobs to pay the bills. Then, in some cases, when a desire is strong and has a profound impact on one's life, there will come a time when that desire cannot be ignored, and the cry of one's soul must be tended to.

This short story is about a woman named Bridget, who tried to ignore her 'creative' calling in exchange for a regular paycheck, until one day she could no longer live the lie. On that day, she faced her reality and made the difficult decision to live her truth.

Following your heart isn't always easy, but if you have a genuine, deep desire to do something you're drawn to and love, it's worth taking the risk and pursuing it. It's said, 'Do what you love, the money will follow; and you will never work a day in your life.'

Monday morning, 5:00 AM, the alarm was beeping. Bridget opened her eyes and stared at the ceiling in despair when something inside her snapped. She could not live this lie another day. Seven years were enough; the truth had to be told today. Dropping to her knees, she prayed for courage and began her day.

In two months, Bridget would celebrate her 30th birthday. She felt terrorized by the approaching milestone and could

think of nothing but living her truth, which she had been avoiding.

Suppressing her life's calling to please her support circle and surrendering to the fear in her mind, she had chosen to exchange her value as an artist for a regular paycheck, doing work she had no interest in. But her life had become a constant misery that consumed her, a burden she could no longer tolerate. The truth had to be spoken, and the consequences had to be faced.

A born artist with extraordinary skills, she excelled in all her art classes and was happiest when she could create, dream up new projects, and connect with her artistic community. Yet she was not living according to her true purpose, and her spirit was slowly dwindling while her soul begged to be freed into the creative world, despite its uncertainties.

Twice a year, she had the privilege of attending art fairs in her community, where she displayed her creations and occasionally sold pieces. Recently, one of the most prestigious art shows was held in her neighborhood. Realizing she had no completed artwork to display, she was deeply disappointed in herself. Yet she attended, tormented by the lie she lived, which prevented her from enjoying the event. This torment reminded her of a hard truth: life could not continue like this.

Bridget had been advised to keep her artistic pursuits as a hobby and focus on a conventional job to support her life. She obeyed, but by the end of each day, she had no energy left to invest in her art. Numerous unfinished pieces were scattered

throughout her living space, evidence of a dying artistic dream —a dream that was dying alongside her soul, until this bright, beautiful Monday morning, just a few days after the prestigious art show was held in her neighborhood.

8:00 AM. At work, sitting in her cubicle, overwhelmed by tedious tasks, she felt the weight of her unfulfilling job. She recalled reading that most heart attacks occur on Monday mornings, the most depressing day of the week. At that moment, she decided—this would not be her story. Reviewing her workload for the day, she realized she would collapse if she did not make a decision soon.

Her cubicle felt like invisible prison walls. Her creative ideas had no respect for her nine-to-five schedule nor her attempts to rest. Inspiration often arrived at the worst times, late at night when she needed sleep, early in the morning during her commute, or midday while she was inundated with projects.

Her job paralyzed her life. She rarely socialized, rushing home each evening to rest and prepare for the next day. Weekends offered little relief: Saturdays were spent recuperating, while Sundays were spent preparing for the workweek. She was dismayed by the compromise she had made for a paycheck.

11:00 AM. Her prayer for courage was answered. She made a decision:

"This is the day! Not just the day, but the hour; and now is the moment!"

Skillfully, she moved her assigned projects to one side of her desk, opened a file drawer containing a few personal items she no longer wanted, disposing of them in the trash bin. She clutched a pen and a notepad, feeling the edges of the paper and admiring the pen as she imagined it writing the ticket to her freedom. Then meticulously, she wrote:

"I have decided to follow my dreams. I can no longer ignore my heart's desire and my soul's calling. Thank you, all, and best wishes."

Placing the note on top of the pile of projects, she picked up her purse and headed toward the elevator, momentarily overwhelmed by the silent voice of fear in her head whispering, "How could you do this?" She glanced around and yelled, "Shut up! Enough of you!"

Then, cheerfully, she stepped into the elevator, pressed the 'L' button, and arrived in the lobby. She walked outside into the bright, sunlit day through large glass doors. Breathing deeply, she felt as if someone had released her from long imprisonment. The sun warmed her face, and a sense of peace washed over her, knowing she had made the right choice.

Her thoughts turned to her dining room, bathed in sunlight all day, a place she loved for reflection and inspiration. Tipsy from her breakout, she thought aloud:

Today, I won't have to breathe recycled office air while people sneeze and cough. I will honor the talent God has placed in me and break these invisible chains. No longer will I allow my soul to be trapped and drained, returning home exhausted night after night to flop onto the bed with the television as my only company. I will not let my life fade into mere survival; I cannot expose my soul to this devastation and deterioration any longer.

Leaving the sunlight, she returned to the lobby after about ten minutes in the sun. Entering the elevator and pressing the 'G' button for the garage.

11:45 AM. With a piercing cry, she declared, "I am moving toward freedom and purpose. I am answering my call, seizing my freedom, and returning to joy. Life never announces the right time to follow your dreams; you have to listen to your inner guide, and mine is ready to live fully."

12:00 PM. She had absconded from the building that had restrained her. She drove to an elegant café she often passed on her lunch breaks, ordered coffee, and sat with her legs crossed, drenched in freedom and on her way to reclaim her dreams.

After having what tasted like the best cup of coffee, she left and headed in the direction of her home.

Arriving home, she was a transformed person from the miserable woman who had left hours before. Looking in the mirror, she saw the woman she once knew, excited to reconnect. Attractive and petite, with shoulder-length brown

wavy hair, bright eyes that match her hair, and an olive complexion that looked pale from not having sun during the day, as she was always locked in at her office. She stretched out on her bed, hugging pillows, thinking, "I am free and unchained; I can return to the purpose of my existence."

Even though she had showered a few hours ago when she prepared for work, she revisited the shower and selected a favorite bar of soap that had never been used. Throwing the old bar in the trash, she washed the job out of her hair, along with all the voices in her head asking her, How can you do this? Then, dressed in her favorite pajamas, she poured a glass of wine, celebrated quietly, and dozed on the sofa, keeping company with a movie and a few television shows, as she celebrated her newfound freedom.

As midnight approached, she felt like a child on Christmas Eve, excited about what might be under the tree for her, as a joyful anticipation filled her. The rest of the week became a celebration of freedom, a reward for taking the steps she had dreamt of throughout her nine-to-five life. She reflected on how to recapture her life's calling.

One week later, in her sunlit dining room, Bridget faced her truth as she sat at her beautiful six-foot mahogany dining table. Surrounded by bookcases and artifacts, it became her creative workspace. She arranged her art supplies within reach, settled herself with her sketchpad, and answered her life's calling.

Five years later, Bridget could not be happier. She moved to a smaller flat to accommodate her income. Her artwork had purpose, and her life had freedom. She had distanced herself from the skeptics. She painted when inspiration flowed, and rested when needed. Art transported her to places of beauty, where she fashioned her creations. Occasionally, financial challenges arose, but she always met her responsibilities. She worked longer hours creating art than she had at her previous job, but now her work feels joyful. Bridget refused to serve a sentence doing a job that was not her calling to pay bills.

She never felt she was working; creating art was like play for her – she told a friend, 'I am playing my way through life,' and that is awesome.

In the art world, she cultivated new relationships, socialized, and promoted her work. She welcomed a few old friends back into her new life, enjoying their respect.

Satisfied with her decision to leave office work, she relished each day and gazed joyfully into the future. After serving her sentence in office, she is very pleased that she no longer has to live a lie.

Painting always brought her joy, and the freedom to manage her schedule allowed her to observe sunrises and sunsets, which she had previously missed due to involuntary distractions. With time to develop her ideas, she created impeccable pieces and was well rewarded for her talent.

Since we all strive for freedom, retirement, and the fulfillment of our personal dreams, why not take the chance

and live our dreams now? Why wait? The future is uncertain, and tomorrow is not promised to anyone; all we truly have is now. Live your dream!

The End

40

NOVELLA

Last Chance for Love

Finding Romance in the Third Act of Life

Author's Note:

A story between two unsuspecting people: a prominent attorney, Andy, and one of his clients, Anne.

Andy was approaching mandatory retirement and was terrified at the idea. To prepare himself, he decided to test what it would feel like to be at home with no work, fully retired, spending his days with his wife of twenty years.

He began taking time off from his job to experience what retirement might be like.

After the first week, however, he grew concerned about being home. His wife already had an established routine that didn't allow for his unexpected presence. Andy began to feel consumed by loneliness and found himself reflecting on life in ways he never had before. He pondered companionship, love, and romance, as well as his ideal place to live and how to spend his free time. Most of all, he wondered how to avoid feeling lonely and isolated.

Andy kept asking himself, "What should I do?" As he wrestled with these questions, he decided to reach out to one of his former clients, Anne, who had become a good friend. She had been living alone for a long time and seemed genuinely happy. At least, she appeared free and lighthearted. Anne owned two homes and seemed to be thriving, enjoying her independence and the freedom to live life on her own terms.

Talking with her opened Andy's eyes to a different way of life—her way of life. Anne had created a fulfilling life for herself, doing what she wanted, when she wanted, and she was fortunate enough to have the choices she did.

Before long, Andy found himself thinking about Anne constantly. Then, speaking to her a few times, he decided to join her on a singles cruise. The experience was exhilarating, and afterward, he wanted to visit her vacation home to see if being there would bring him the same joy she always described. Anne had often spoken about the Caribbean town where her cottage was located, painting it as a picture-perfect paradise. Andy wanted to experience it for himself.

After the cruise, he spent a week with Anne at her vacation cottage. That trip, along with the cruise, gave Andy a new perspective on life. He realized he was longing for certain things in his marriage that his wife wasn't providing. After several unsuccessful attempts to persuade her to join him in various activities, he decided to compile a list of questions to better understand how she envisioned retirement and whether her vision aligned with his.

Andy was gathering information to make a conscious decision about the final act of his life. To him, life unfolded in three stages: the first act, from birth to thirty; the second act, from thirty to sixty; and the third and final act, from sixty until the end of life.

This story is about making conscious choices, adapting to change, and aligning with your current circumstances and

needs. It is about adjusting to *life as it is now*. In the twenty-first century, you cannot be successful in the business world with only a facsimile machine and a typewriter—times have changed. In today's world, refusing to use modern technology risks leaving you behind, facing frustration and defeat.

I hope you enjoy this story about the 'journey of life' – showcasing our varying needs at different stages.

JRam

Last Chance for Love

Andy's Sneak Peek Into Retirement

Up until his last birthday, everything about Andy's life had felt perfect. But the day after his birthday, he woke up with an unfamiliar sense of emptiness and fear at the thought of retirement looming in a few years. That's when he began exploring how he truly wanted to live in this next chapter. He realized he didn't want his life to stay the same; he craved something different.

Andy started questioning himself: *Do I have to retire, sit still, and let myself wither away? Or can I still have love, romance, excitement, and joy in my later years?*

And so, Andy's journey began…

Our needs evolve with each life stage, which is natural, as the needs we had as teenagers differ from those at forty or fifty. While some interests may still attract us, it's crucial to continue growing from one stage to the next.

Once, I heard a young couple with their eight-month-old baby say to a pastor, "I wish she would stay like this all her

life." The pastor replied, "No, that would not be good. Pray that she grows beautifully through each stage of her life!"

Life is about growth. When we study nature, we see how easily this unfolds. For example, a young seedling requires different care than a mature plant, just as a baby needs different care from a ten-year-old child.

Andy Lord, a prominent attorney, was preparing for his Third Act. As he began planning for retirement, he realized that many of the things he now desires were missing from his life. As a result, he became petrified to move forward with the mandatory retirement plan—a plan he himself helped establish at the very law firm he helped build.

As retirement approached, fear about the future consumed Andy. He could not imagine living the same way he and his wife had for the past twenty years.

One day, he decided to speak openly with his wife about his concerns and the new desires he had begun to cultivate. He was sharing how his needs were evolving. That discussion, however, put him in an uphill battle, leaving him at a crossroads where he had to choose.

Andy yearns for a different kind of love than what he's grown accustomed to. He craves romance, passion, and excitement. But can he achieve that?

He wonders, *"Is it selfish to choose life and love for my Third Act? Or should I remain in a mundane situation that lacks joy and wait to take my last breath?"*

After twenty years of a comfortable marriage, Andy woke up the morning after his fifty-fifth birthday celebration feeling unsettled. Retirement was only a few years away, and he realized the life he was living—and the future he envisioned—were not what he wanted.

He needed to retire at sixty, but the prospect of the next five years filled him with dread. To ease his anxiety, he decided to give himself one year to plan his retirement and put everything into perspective with his firm. During that time, he focused on training his shadow attorney, occasionally stepping away from work to experience a break. He called this his 'retirement testing.'

In the first three months of his planning and 'retirement testing,' Andy spent time at home with his wife, who had stopped working a few years earlier. She had grown unhappy maintaining a career while leaving their home to be managed by housekeepers and other staff. She felt she should be home, enjoying the life they had built and personally overseeing its management. After discussing her concerns with Andy, he fully supported her decision, and she began living her 'best life,' managing their home and enjoying the freedom to do as she pleased.

On the first day of Andy's retirement testing, he experienced his wife's lifestyle firsthand and was impressed by how fulfilled she seemed. However, by the second day, a sobering realization struck him: there was no real place for him in her world at home. He felt like an intruder. His wife had a structured schedule filled with activities, including spending

time with friends and family, as well as coordinating with housekeepers, gardeners, repair personnel, and everyone else involved in maintaining their elaborate home.

Although Andy and his wife never had children, her close ties with family and friends kept her days completely occupied. While he appreciated the comfort of their well-maintained home, he began to feel like an outsider in his own space. The thought of being home full-time after retirement unsettled him deeply. After struggling for about a week to express his feelings, often unsure of exactly how he felt, he began retreating more often to his private study.

In many ways, Andy was confined to his study, effectively placed in a decorative box within his own home. It was beautiful and meticulously maintained, resembling a museum room, yet he found comfort in it. His study became a sanctuary where he could work, read, think, and, most importantly, stay out of his wife's way.

Although Andy had spent time at home during his career, he had never viewed it the way he did now. For the first time, he was forced to confront the reality of the next phase of his life, the 'third act,' the final chapter. Without his career to occupy his mind, he feared losing the sense of purpose that had defined him for decades. His work had consumed much of his time, and he loved it.

Early in the second week of his 'retirement testing,' Andy decided to attend a conference he had been debating attending for months. Staying home made him feel misplaced, so leaving

seemed like the better option. When he told his wife he'd be away for a week, she said, "Okay, honey." She didn't ask where he was going, why, or for how long. Realizing this indifference was typical for her, he moved forward with his plans, grateful for the distraction.

Andy increasingly felt that his only role in maintaining their lifestyle was paying the bills. One afternoon, he sat quietly in his office for nearly three hours, ignoring calls and reflecting on how mechanical his life had become. The thought that retirement would mean more of this hollow routine deeply troubled him.

The only consistent time his wife spent with him was during their thirty-minute breakfasts and their evening dinners in the elegant, carefully curated dining room. His wife disliked traveling and was perfectly content staying home, surrounded by everything she loved, enjoying the freedom and comfort of her chosen lifestyle. That arrangement had worked for years, but Andy now realized it wouldn't work for him as a retiree. Work had always kept him busy, even after hours, when he often brought projects home or took calls from clients across different time zones. In hindsight, he recognized his role in creating the 'elephant' that not only lingered in the room but had come to dominate their entire household and way of life.

After dinner, Andy would typically unwind in his recliner in the beautifully decorated sitting room, while his wife busied herself around the house, tending to things she adored. Yet he often sat there feeling invisible. After about two hours, she

would kiss him gently on the forehead and retire to her separate bedroom, a routine that unsettled him deeply.

Sleeping in Separate Beds

When his wife had stopped working, she decided to move into her own bedroom. She had explained her reasons clearly, emphasizing that her late-night habits might disturb his sleep. She had her own schedule and believed this arrangement was best for them. Although Andy disliked the idea, he agreed, wanting her to be happy.

Such an arrangement was complicated for Andy, bringing him significant discomfort. Still, to please his wife, he agreed to it after negotiating that they would regularly sleep in the same bedroom. Over the years, however, even that agreement eventually faded. Now, Andy was left feeling lonely in the love department. He knew his wife loved him, but after twenty years of marriage, he thought she was no longer **in love** with him.

Andy longed for love and romance. In his mid-fifties, he was still a vibrant man, yet he felt forced to live a dormant life that was becoming increasingly burdensome, especially with retirement looming. His thoughts became consumed with the idea of retiring, just as he had once been consumed with his career and, later, his marriage.

Being around women and dealing with matters of love had always been challenging for Andy because he was naturally very shy. He felt as though it had been a handicap since his

youth. In high school and college, he had hardly dated, and he eventually met his wife in graduate school, where a short courtship led to marriage by the time they graduated. In the early days of their relationship, his wife had been the pursuer, pushing for them to be together.

Andy was the type of person who focused intensely on his studies and would have gladly dedicated all his energy to his career. Yet he chose to share his life with his wife and had been happy until now. His reserved way of life had left him with almost no experience in dating, and he often felt incapable of wining and dining women. For twenty years, he had been content in his marriage. But now, as he evaluated the reality of his upcoming retirement, he felt an overwhelming emptiness.

There seemed to be nothing to look forward to. Travel, something he had always dreamed of, became complicated. His wife was afraid of flying and sailing; she felt an unshakable need to remain on solid ground. To her, the air and sea belonged to birds and fish—not people. But Andy couldn't imagine limiting himself to trains or buses. His life felt fixed in place, and the thought of living this way for the rest of his years was traumatizing.

Andy was experiencing a deep, unfamiliar loneliness. He began longing for someone to share his concerns and private thoughts with. For a while, he considered seeing a therapist, but another thought surfaced—one about a former client who had always stayed in touch. Her name was Anne, a lovely and vibrant woman with an effortlessly charming outlook on life.

He found himself wondering how she was, where she might be, and what she was doing. Over the years, their communication had been minimal—usually exchanging New Year's greetings and perhaps a phone call or two to say "Hello." Yet, a week later, Andy realized he couldn't stop thinking about her. It dawned on him that Anne had been the one client he had genuinely liked. After some deliberation, he decided he would call her.

Reconnecting With A Former Client

It had been about a month since Andy's birthday, and his thoughts about his potential, possibly mundane retirement were beginning to lessen, even though it was still five years away — well, slightly less than five years now.

As the new month began, he received a message from his former client, Anne, whom he had been thinking about recently. Anne had been referred to him by a colleague who had left the firm years ago. From the very beginning, Anne captivated Andy with her energy and her refreshing outlook on life. In addition, she was attractive and full of joy, making her even more enchanting. She had a free spirit, yet when it came to her legal matters, she handled everything with utmost seriousness and professionalism. She knew exactly what she wanted from life and was quietly, yet deliberately, moving in that direction.

Andy had worked with her for about three years, successfully resolving a legal issue. He saw her roughly five

times during that period, and each meeting was a pleasure for him, in the most professional way.

Anne was an architect and interior designer who ran her own business, traveling extensively across the country and internationally. She was several years younger than Andy. After her case was resolved, he had told her to stay in touch, and she did. She would check in two or three times a year, especially around Christmas or at the start of the New Year, to wish him well.

Andy always felt good hearing from Anne. Each time she reached out, it felt as though she infused him with some of her positive energy, and he loved it. After about three years of this occasional communication and considering where he found himself in life, he felt the need to connect with her on a deeper level. So, when he received her recent message, he was genuinely excited.

Hearing from her delighted him, especially since he had been thinking about her during a time when he longed for meaningful conversation. Receiving her message brought a certain lightness to his otherwise complicated feelings. He sat for a while, letting his mind wander as curiosity took over. He wondered: Did she have a husband or a significant other? Did she have children, and if so, how many? How was she doing? How was she always so upbeat? What is her life like now?

Andy kept thinking about Anne, not romantically or sexually, but as a cherished friend. He was a faithful husband, and besides that, his shy and somewhat reserved nature made

flirting unthinkable. What he wanted was to extend their friendship, perhaps have more regular communication, and maybe arrange a lunch together when their schedules allowed. He longed for someone he could trust, someone he could have genuine conversations with, and he felt comfortable with her in a way that was rare for him. He also wanted to know more about her, viewing his intentions as pure and respectful.

Since Anne was always the one initiating contact, sending greetings and holiday cards, Andy felt perfectly fine about returning the gesture. He asked his assistant to schedule a call with her as soon as possible. When his assistant reached out, however, Anne was unavailable until the following week.

On the day of the scheduled call, Andy dressed immaculately, despite having no in-person client appointments or meetings. He was visibly excited, prompting his assistant to ask what the matter was. He smiled and said, "I'm feeling good!"

At the appointed time, the call came through, and Andy picked up immediately.

"Andy, how the heck are you?" Anne's voice was warm and lively.

"Great!" he replied. "What about you? How are you, and where are you? I understand you were too busy to take my call the other day."

"I was traveling until two days ago," she explained, "but I'm at my country cottage now, in the Cayman Islands. I'm taking this call sitting under my 100-year-old Tamarind tree in

the backyard. Andy, I'm communing with nature and grounding myself."

He chuckled. "Are you really sitting on the dirt under a tree?"

"Absolutely," she said. "Right on the dirt, with my back against the tree's trunk. I used to pay so much money to go on retreats to do exactly this; now I do it here for free, and for as long as I want."

"I can only imagine how that feels," he said. "So, is your husband there, enjoying this with you?"

She laughed softly. "He wishes. You see, he divorced me a few years back. Now he calls me all the time, wanting us to get back together, but I'm not leaning in that direction."

"Oh, I see," Andy said gently.

She continued, "We didn't have children, the divorce was amicable, and honestly, I'm happy. My ex-husband thought leaving the marriage would make him happier, but now he realizes it didn't."

Andy shifted the conversation. "When will you be in my neck of the woods? I'd love to invite you to lunch so we can sit and talk for a bit."

"I'm not quite sure when I'll be coming to New York," Anne replied, "but I will be traveling next week. I'll let you know if I can arrange a layover that would allow us to meet."

She paused briefly, then added, "Actually… I think I can make it possible. I'll let you know tomorrow."

"Great! I'll look out for your call," he said warmly. "Enjoy the rest of your day sitting on the dirt."

She laughed and said, "You should try it someday."

He chuckled, and they ended the call. Andy felt like he could hop and skip, but he wondered, what was it about her that captivated him so deeply?

Anne wasn't mechanical or robotic like many of the people Andy interacted with daily. She was infused with natural spontaneity, perhaps developed over the course of her life as a designer, architect, and only child. She seemed quick to laugh at herself, at life, and at little absurdities. She viewed the world through lenses different from those of the attorneys Andy had spent his career surrounded by, and she was very different from his wife. He wondered what she enjoyed doing, how she maintained her positive attitude as a single person, and what her secret to that was. Overall, he wanted to know more about her because she was the only client he kept thinking about long after her case was closed.

Later that day, Anne reviewed her travel plans and realized she could book a connecting flight that included a few hours' layover in New York. She decided to take that option, allowing herself to meet Andy for lunch. She told herself that if it worked for Andy, that would be great, and if not, she would use the time at the airport productively, catching up on projects and making a few calls.

The next day, she phoned Andy's assistant and shared the details of her new travel itinerary. When Andy reviewed the

plans, he thought they were perfect as he would be able to step away from his conference for a few hours to meet her. He called her directly and confirmed their lunch.

"I'll cover any extra expenses you incur for coming out of the airport to meet me," he offered.

"Thank you!" she said warmly. "I'm looking forward to seeing you."

Andy was purposefully joyful about this reconnection with Anne. He was excited to see her, eager for their conversation, and hopeful that their meeting would give him a fresh perspective on his life and the decisions ahead.

Andy's Conference - Meets Anne

The following week seemed to take forever to arrive. While waiting for his upcoming trip and the chance to reconnect with Anne, one night, he tried to persuade his wife to join him in some romantic pleasures. She refused and acted as if his request was entirely out of character. Disheartened, he retreated to his room, reflecting deeply on his life, yet he struggled to find any answers that brought him comfort.

When the conference finally arrived, Andy found himself far more interested in seeing Anne than participating in the event itself. She was the highlight of his week, while the conference felt dull and uninspiring by comparison.

The day of Anne's visit finally came, and Andy felt like a ten-year-old receiving a brand-new bike. They agreed to meet

at his hotel, where they would choose one of the several restaurants available. Over lunch, they enjoyed lively conversations, endless laughter, and an effortless connection. Anne told Andy she felt as though they were old friends reunited after many years, and the chemistry between them was undeniable.

After three hours together, Anne left for the airport, realizing she genuinely liked him not just as her attorney but as a person, and that they could build a real friendship. Andy, meanwhile, was left carrying the warmth of her positive energy, already wondering when he might next be graced with her company.

Anne is a realist. She spends no time on 'maybe.' She does what makes her feel good and what is right, understanding that people need different things for comfort and personal growth at various stages of life.

Andy could not stop thinking about Anne and her captivating outlook on life. She was spontaneous and fun, possessed an impressive sense of humor, and radiated love, warmth, and kindness. He noticed how people were naturally drawn to her and eager to do things for her, and she treated everyone with respect and sound judgment.

Anne had told him that she found it challenging to live alone in one home as she matured. Her love for gardening, visiting local markets, and the idea of having a second place to call home — somewhere she could go whenever she pleased, with warm weather year-round — was deeply fulfilling. It

gave her the feeling of being on vacation all the time, or of being able to have a vacation whenever she wanted, in a place with her own stuff —a place she loved.

She enjoyed planning her trips between her homes, always preparing something to do or shop for at each location. Most of the time, she coordinated her travels so that leaving one home and returning to the other flowed seamlessly. She loved cooking and eating seasonal foods from each area, feeling blessed to have made friends in both locations. If no one she knew was available, especially at her vacation home, she would spend time with the locals instead.

Anne often visited piano bars, as there were a couple within walking distance of her cottage. When she wanted to venture farther, a short taxi ride was all it took. She enjoyed dressing up, dining out, and being serenaded by piano music, often performed by local musicians, which brought her great joy.

Andy now found himself imagining life with a woman like Anne: sitting together in the garden, traveling from home to home, shopping for their spaces, cooking and eating seasonal dishes, visiting local markets, and mingling with the locals. Anne had once mentioned that she sometimes wished for someone to accompany her to various events, especially at her vacation home, someone to hold hands with, stroll along the beautiful cobblestone streets, sit together on benches, share an ice cream cone, and appreciate the simple "beauty of life". Her primary home, however, was mostly business as usual, and she didn't feel that same yearning there.

Andy had little recollection of the rest of his conference, which passed like a blur because his thoughts were consumed by Anne's company, her laughter, and her perspective on life. He couldn't get enough of her.

Anne, on the other hand, had long admired Andy in his role as her attorney. Over the years, they had built a strong client-attorney relationship, and now she appreciated the shift toward friendship. She held tremendous respect for marriage, especially for the role of a wife, and had no desire to cause anyone pain, believing firmly that what goes around comes around. She was happy to deepen their friendship, but was clear with herself that it would never be more than that.

She set aside any other thoughts about Andy, telling herself that he would undoubtedly be an excellent catch if he were single. For now, though, she was content: they would be good friends, and that was enough. Everything was good—perfect.

Andy - Returning Home After The Conference

Andy's conference concluded, and he began his journey home. During his connecting flight, he had about an hour before boarding the next plane and found himself observing couples around his age. It struck him that everyone seemed happier than he was. The fear of retirement weighed heavily on him with each passing thought, fueled by his assumption that all these couples had more fulfilling lives than his own.

Then another thought crossed his mind: *If Anne were here with me at this airport, we would look like a happy couple.* He realized that not all the people he saw were couples; some might be siblings, close friends, or even coworkers. Still, he held on to the energy Anne left him, an energy that was both intriguing and uplifting, fueling his wishful thoughts of meeting her to spend more time with her. But reality pulled him back; he had to return home to his life.

Arriving home brought no excitement. No one seemed glad to see him. He even thought about getting a dog, but his wife disliked dogs, which made that idea impossible. He wondered if, had he not come home when he said he would, it would have even caused a problem, or if anyone would have even missed him. So, he did what was expected of him: he had dinner with his wife, which was as uneventful as ever, and then settled into his recliner. From there, he looked around at their well-maintained home while his wife busied herself for about two hours before kissing him on the forehead and heading to her bedroom.

That night, he tried once more to get her attention, hoping she would cuddle and spend time with him, but she brushed him off as she had been doing for a long time. Eventually, he went to bed alone, his thoughts drifting to Anne. He wondered what she might be doing at that very moment and whether she had reached her destination. Not knowing for sure, he decided to send her a message to say "Hello," letting her know how happy he was about their meeting, and asked her to sync up when she had time.

The following evening, as he got into bed, Andy found himself wondering why Anne hadn't responded yet. He decided to send her another text, asking what she was doing and if she was okay. About thirty minutes later, her reply came.

"Hi Andy, I am fine, and you may not want to know what I am doing, but I will tell you since you asked. On my way to the hotel yesterday, I bought a bunch of pink roses, and now I'm dismantling them and placing the petals on the bed so I can lie on a bed of roses."

Andy could only imagine why her husband would want to rush back to her, because he wanted to be there too, not for sex, but for the sheer experience of lying on rose petals and being in her company. Smiling faintly, he responded.

"Anne, I have no words for you… You are intriguing. Enjoy your night and sweet dreams."

He put down his phone and felt lonelier than ever. In that quiet moment, he clearly understood why so many married men end up in adulterous relationships, not that he didn't understand that before, but it seemed so right in this moment, that it's the right thing to do – Andy was not in a good state of mind.

Why Do Couples Who Are Bored with Life And Each Other Stay Together?

When people fall out of love, why do they remain together? It's interesting, but many could avoid tremendous hurt, illness, and even tragedy by leaving amicably.

Anne often played a game in her mind, observing couples and wondering whether she could distinguish the happy ones from those who had lost the joy of being together. She was convinced it was easy to spot the difference. The couples who had endured decades together often carried burdensome expressions and a lack of joy. In contrast, the happy ones carried the radiance of being agreeable with one another, holding hands and smiling as they went about.

She felt the unhappy ones were drained by disappointments in a life they had built together that no longer worked. Perhaps years of disrespect, poor communication, lost trust, family conflicts, infidelity, disloyalty, regrets, setbacks, and the fading of love had left them empty, making their exhaustion evident in their facial expressions and body language.

Looking at them, she felt that the absence of love and romance had turned into disgust, and contempt had replaced affection. Anne believed they spent their days silently shooting 'poisoned arrows' at each other, harboring resentment and wishing they had chosen a different partner and a different lifestyle.

It seems clear that some grew angry that they were still bound by an agreement made when things were different, back when happiness was plentiful and the world seemed full of promise. Now, it looked as though that same world was pressing down on them, suffocating their dreams and what's left of life. When they should be in a state of peaceful reflection on a life well lived, they appear to dislike, or even

hate one another, for what they have not achieved, blaming the other for missed opportunities, misfortune, and the responsibilities that weigh them down. Many began to see their partner as a burden, and in darker moments, some even wished the other would vanish.

This is why, when someone disappears or is killed, investigators often look first to the significant other. No one can hate a person more deeply than a partner who once loved them but now feels trapped and betrayed. That invisible prison, the longing to be freed from a life they no longer want, can become the unspoken motive behind acts of desperation, even murder.

The combined energies of many couples are 'dead' because they've spent years learning to live with disappointments, hiding their pain behind forced smiles, and carrying on when what they truly needed was to cry, heal, and move on.

Then we have those who lead stagnant lives, trying to prove they are stable, but they don't truly thrive, and happiness is a distant memory for them. But they remain because it's financially easier.

Some honor the expectations of others: their children and grandchildren, in-laws, extended family, friends, neighbors, and society itself. There's the house they've built, the life they've shared, and the unspoken pressure to maintain appearances.

Leaving is rarely the norm and is often seen as unacceptable. Many watched their parents die a little each day in marriages that drained their spirit and killed their souls, until their final breath. Yet they follow that example, believing they must endure the same fate.

In truth, countless people die emotionally long before they are officially pronounced dead—some have been 'gone' for years, but they still smile and maintain the appearance of what used to be or could have been.

Anne shared with Andy that many of the happy older couples were not in lifelong marriages. Most had remarried after divorce or widowhood, or they had married for the first time later in life. And when you see them, it's a joyful feeling that there is still a chance for love.

Andy Fell In Love

Andy wondered if Anne would have an affair with him. Still, reality instantly visited him to let him know that if he did such a thing, he would have to stay with her, because he would never be able to return to his mechanical life after having experienced something with her. However, Anne seemed reserved and clear about what she wanted. If she were a more aggressive woman who did not hold such deep respect for marriage, that might have happened easily.

As he thought about it further, he realized it wasn't the affair he was yearning for; it was the fun and excitement Anne brought into everything she did. That was what he craved, that

was what he was drawn to, and that was what he was truly in love with. He admitted to himself that he would have to be free before suggesting anything like that to Anne.

He wasn't even sure if she would be interested in a man like him. By most standards, he was what people called a 'stiff shirt.' A powerful attorney, with an abundance of height, and good-looking, yet serious to the point of intimidating others. His shyness kept him reserved, and his lack of a sense of humor made him seem unapproachable. He was tunnel-focused on his work, rarely allowing himself to step outside his rigid routine.

Andy admired Anne and the way she lived her life. During lunch at his conference, she explained how she viewed existence. She said, "From the day you are born to the day you die, life is a dash in time. What are you doing with your dash? Will you let your life be defined by a decision you made in your youth, one that no longer works for you now that you are older? Should you still be investing in the car you loved back in college? Would it be effective in today's world of technology, where cars can drive themselves and park autonomously? Would it really fit your life now?"

She paused before continuing. "I'm not suggesting we treat people like objects, but we need to be honest with ourselves and evaluate what is working and what isn't. Then, we must make wise decisions. If you're unhappy, choose to be happy, even if that means learning to love what you already have. And if you can't love what you have and you have countless

reasons why you cannot leave…Then, I suppose, you'll have to pretend. Life is short, and there are no rehearsals."

Anne was spontaneous and very imaginative; she once told him she could go anywhere in her mind and create scenes as if her mind had visions of other places. Andy found himself wondering if it was possible to have an intimate relationship with Anne that didn't involve sex. To him, sex was merely a by-product of intimacy, sometimes even an obstacle to it. What he wanted was excitement in his life, a chance to experience something different, something vibrant, like what Anne was living. And he understood that she hadn't reached this place easily; she had been forced to make difficult choices along the way.

Intimacy had been scarce in Andy's life for an exceptionally long time. Even during moments of physical closeness with his wife, there had been no real connection between them for many years. Now, after only a few interactions with Anne, he felt an unfamiliar sense of intimacy with her and found himself longing for her time, her presence, and her attention.

A week later, he called her, and she was at her main home in Connecticut, enjoying some quiet time. She had traveled extensively over the past two weeks, so she said she planned to stay home and practice some 'selective solitude,' avoiding dinners out or social events. She mentioned that the following weekend, she was heading to Bermuda for a few days, a trip she had planned long ago. "I love Bermuda and its beaches," she said, her voice warm with anticipation. "After visiting

there about five years ago, I loved it so much that I look forward to visiting every year at least once."

Back in his office, immersed in his structured life, Andy asked where she was going after Bermuda. She told him that next, she would be taking a singles cruise through the Mediterranean for a week, departing from London. After that, she planned to settle in for the next six weeks. She confessed that, "Lately, I have been thinking it might be nice to share my joyful life with someone I was truly compatible with. And if that doesn't happen, she added with a laugh, I'll settle for a puppy."

She had even started contemplating what kind of puppy she might want. She'd never owned one before, but several of her friends had, and they seemed genuinely happy with their little companions.

Going On A Singles Cruise - Looking For Love

Learning about the 'singles cruise' Anne was planning, Andy grew bold and asked if he could accompany her. She quickly reminded him that it was intended for singles, but then admitted that technically, anyone could go.

Andy said, "I will come on the cruise and get my own private suite so I can spend time rethinking life. This would also give me the chance to do things alongside you, if you'd like." He further explained that he would be happy just being on the same ship as her and promised he would not impose on

her in any way. He wanted to try something different, have fun, and figure out the next chapter of his life. The thought of having someone he already knew on board made the idea much more appealing and less intimidating.

"I have traveled the world for my work and have no problem doing so. In fact, I function well that way," he said. "But when it comes to going out on certain occasions, I sometimes feel uncomfortable."

She replied, "I'll send you the information. If you're serious, you'll need to act quickly, as I hear the cruise is almost sold out."

That same day, Andy booked his spot on the cruise without telling anyone. He handled the booking himself because he didn't want his assistant involved. When he told his wife that he had to travel for business, she responded, as usual, "Okay, honey."

The week before the cruise, Anne checked in with Andy, who then told her he was fully booked and ready to go. She was surprised and realized he was serious, so she expressed to him how much she was looking forward to seeing him and spending quality time together on the ship.

As the departure date approached, Anne grew increasingly excited about the fun she anticipated during the week of sailing and exploring several Mediterranean cities.

However, after Andy confirmed his booking, Anne hadn't heard from him for a few days. On the day of the cruise, she boarded the ship in London, having arrived two days earlier.

She loved London and used the time to stroll through its charming streets, window-shop, and indulge in ice cream for dessert after a delicious dinner at one of the restaurants near her hotel.

Once she boarded the ship and began exploring, she didn't see Andy anywhere and wondered if he had decided not to come after all, thinking perhaps he had only been joking. But about an hour later, while mingling and waiting to access her room, she finally spotted him. Both were excited to see each other again. Anne suggested they head to the upper deck to watch the water and take in the view while they waited for their rooms and luggage to be ready.

On The Cruise

"I will not be able to spend significant time with you as I'll be looking around and mingling," Anne whispered. Andy nodded in agreement. After cocktails, their rooms were finally ready, and they went their separate ways to get settled in for their week of cruising, planning to return for dinner in their allotted dining rooms at 7 p.m.

Anne was a vision of beauty as she walked to her assigned table. Being average height and weight, she looked stunning in anything she wore, but then, it was her inner beauty that always shone forth.

Seated at a table for six, three people were already there: two men and a woman, all pleasant-looking and nicely dressed. People always strive to make a good impression on

the first night. That is also when the seating assignments were made so passengers could meet their designated servers. After that evening, everyone was free to sit wherever they wished. They could also return to their original seats if they preferred.

Andy was happy to be alone in his room on the ship. He was on vacation, there to have fun, to see, and spend time with Anne as much as she would allow. He liked the way he was feeling; the world was at his feet, and there was an uplifting energy on the ship. All the other times he had been in hotel rooms were for business, and the times he traveled with his wife were mechanical and uncomfortable, as she disliked travel, making the experience unpleasant for both of them. But now, he was alone, with Anne somewhere on the ship, and he couldn't be happier.

Andy got dressed and went to his assigned dining room. He felt a little lost until he spotted Anne. He mingled briefly with a few women at his table, and they engaged him in conversation. That interaction opened his eyes to how different things felt now; women seemed far bolder and more forward than he was used to. He didn't like that. He preferred to pursue someone he was genuinely attracted to, even if a woman expressed interest in him first, but he disliked overt aggressiveness. He felt that some of the women he encountered on the cruise seemed more interested in his financial worth than in him as a person. That was why his thoughts kept returning to Anne. She had never pursued him and still didn't. She enjoyed an upgraded friendship in which they were both free to share as much or as little as they wanted.

After that first night, Andy decided to be more reserved when sharing personal details. He wasn't there to find companionship; he was there to sort out his life. He was still married, so when asked about his work, he said, "I am in law enforcement," and left it at that.

Andy was amazed by how bold and forward some women were, and while it made him uncomfortable, he welcomed the experience. He believed there was always something to learn from every encounter, and he viewed these interactions as part of his 'retirement testing,' a way to gather information to help him decide on the next phase of his life.

He admitted to himself that he had lived a very structured life. He wasn't complaining, but he couldn't help making comparisons and reflecting on what he wanted the next chapter to look like, as this was his third act. He treated this cruise experience as a kind of research, thinking, "If I want to learn how to swim, I have to get in the water."

As the evening progressed, he hadn't seen much of Anne, but eventually, after wandering around and pondering his thoughts, he found her on the dance floor. She was having a wonderful time, dancing to lively Latin American music with a group of energetic men and women. Andy took a seat nearby and watched. He felt like he was missing out on this part of life, yet he realized he didn't have to; he wasn't that old. Being around Anne made him feel young and alive.

He wished he could share this sense of freedom and fun with his wife at this stage of their lives. Retirement, he

believed, should represent the freedom we work toward all our lives, not a rehearsal for death, not a time to sit and rot. It should be a time to do what you enjoy, free from the demands of a career, raising children, managing a business, and countless other responsibilities. Many people downsize into smaller homes to reduce the maintenance required in a larger house. Then, some move to warmer climates to free themselves from weather-related burdens, such as frigid cold temperatures, snow and its removal, icy sidewalks, and the burden of wearing layers of clothing to stay warm. Retirement, to Andy, was about transitioning from doing what you *had* to do to doing what you *wanted* to do.

Andy's wife was so mechanical and set in her ways that he had fallen into a mundane, mechanical existence himself alongside her. He was no longer enjoying it, and he knew if he had to continue living this way, he needed a different life plan. Yes, he still had to finish his career over the next few years, but he refused to stay home afterward, sitting in a corner, wasting away. There was too much to rethink.

He began to consider the possibilities open to him after retirement, such as becoming a law professor or opening a private practice. Both ideas felt promising, but they would only occupy his daytime hours. What about the evenings? That's when his loneliness weighed on him the most. He got tired of asking his wife to spend time with him and being refused. He felt that being romantic with your spouse should not be a continuous fight. His wife was done with being intimate with him, and he did not want to accept that reality.

Andy was flexible and wanted something different. Quietly, he noted to himself, *This is where men step out of their marriages.* He wasn't looking for another woman to replace his wife, but he had developed feelings for Anne. She was a few years Andy's junior, and he was pleased that his feelings for her had developed naturally. He thought it was instinctive, this energy, this attraction, this desire to pursue a woman. It was the "chase," the "hunt," something he believed God had placed in men by design.

Third Night Cruising

On the third night of this seven-night cruise, during dinnertime, Andy decided he would dine at the same table as Anne. If that were not possible because the table was already full, then she would have to join him at another table. As he suspected, when he approached her table, it was completely occupied, with two extra men hovering nearby, trying to negotiate with others to exchange seats. They couldn't get enough of Anne, and Andy understood precisely what they were going through, as he was experiencing the same thing.

Wanting to be spontaneous, Andy said to Anne, "Let's take a walk around and see where else we can dine." She replied with a laugh, "Yes, we may even end up eating a burger and fries at a bar!" Her playful response made Andy feel good about his decision. Off they went, strolling through the ship, admiring its beauty, and talking about the incredible engineering behind a floating city. They marveled at the ship's exquisite architectural designs, and as an architect, Anne was

captivated. She grew more excited, pointing out intricate details to Andy as they walked.

After a while, Anne smiled and said, "It looks like we'll have to settle for fried chicken and fries, and I'll love that. How about you?" Andy nodded in agreement, replying, "This is impressive." She laughed and said, "Yes, it's wonderful! But, for eating like this, we must dance for one full hour afterward, without stopping. That's how I do it and that's an order!"

They enjoyed their crispy fried chicken and fries, smothered in generous amounts of ketchup and mustard, then took a long walk around the ship's deck before heading to a club to dance. While walking, Anne turned to Andy and said softly, "This is when I wish I had a partner to hold hands with, maybe even stop for a kiss during a walk like this." Andy smiled warmly and replied, "Anne, you deserve all that and more." She gazed at him thoughtfully and said, "Andy, by now you must realize that I am in love with living my life." He smiled in return as they reached the dance floor, where they spent time dancing, followed by another stroll around the deck, completing their playful 'excuse' for indulging in fried food.

The next day, as the ship pulled into its designated port, Anne was precisely where she loved to be early in the morning during any cruise, on the outer deck. She enjoyed watching the sunrise and planning her day in the city ahead. The night before, as she was 'kissing the evening goodbye,' she had told Andy about her plan to wake up early to see the sunrise and watch the ship dock. "It's a beautiful scene to take in," she said. To her surprise, Andy joined her, and together they

watched the glowing sunrise and admired the splendid views of a new city before breakfast.

At breakfast, Anne teased him, saying, "You must eat only green things and drink green juices." By the end of the meal, passengers were preparing to disembark for tours, sightseeing, and beach excursions. Andy wanted to explore but didn't want to do it alone. He asked Anne about her plans, and she expressed her interest in spending time at the beach, though she didn't mind doing some sightseeing first. Looking at him, she asked what he wanted to do. He replied, "I'd like to do some sightseeing, and I'd love to go to the beach with you."

Anne laughed and said, "Then you'd better get your swimming gear and meet me back here as soon as possible." Andy grinned and said, "I want to be spontaneous. I'll buy new swimwear once we get to the beach." Anne smiled, nodding in approval. "Cool. I'm ready. Let's go see which bus we'll take for the sightseeing tour."

They left the ship along with a few others who had been hovering around Anne. Choosing a comfortable, air-conditioned bus, they enjoyed a few hours of pleasant exploration of the city before being dropped off at the beach. Surprisingly, many of the passengers who hadn't planned on visiting the beach decided to join them there.

Once at the beach, Anne helped Andy shop for swimwear. She noticed he was hesitant in making his selection, which made her smile. It was clear he was the kind of man who usually let his wife handle such decisions, a quality she quietly

admired. To herself, she thought, *"He's still trainable and so adorable... but he's taken."*

On the beach, Anne wanted sunscreen on her back but didn't want Andy to apply it; she felt it would be too personal. Instead, she spent most of her time lying on her back, applying sunscreen to the exposed areas of her body —her front, arms, and legs. Meanwhile, Andy took a walk along the shore while Anne relaxed and watched the clouds drift by. They had a wonderfully enjoyable day. Returning to the ship later, they treated themselves to ice cream cones and lounged poolside. Anne indulged in two cones before they finally returned to their rooms.

Andy walked back to his cabin singing that old Frank Sinatra song, softly, *"You make me feel so young, you make me feel that spring has sprung..."* After showering, he spread a large towel over the bed and lay down unclothed, a rare indulgence for him. He let the water drip from his body onto the towel, and hours later, he woke up feeling refreshed and excited for the night ahead.

Fourth Night Cruising

That evening, Andy made sure to arrive early at Anne's table and waited patiently for her. The wait was worth it; Anne looked stunning, radiant, and full of life. By now, many passengers had paired off and were making plans to spend the evenings together. Andy and Anne enjoyed dinner at her

original table and capped off the evening with a live Broadway show.

During the performance, an emotional scene caught Anne off guard, and without thinking, she reached for Andy's hand. He held her gently, and when she realized what she had done, she looked at him apologetically. Andy smiled and said softly, "That's not necessary." She returned his smile, comforted by his response.

After the show, Anne said, "There are several different restaurants on this ship, and we still have a few nights left. Let's make reservations at a different one for each of the remaining nights." Andy readily agreed. Then Anne added playfully, "Andy, you do realize I've been spending all my time with you, and that defeats the purpose of this trip. You'll need to reimburse me for the cost of this cruise, because I didn't pay all this money to spend it with you, even though I *am* enjoying it."

Andy burst out laughing so hard he had to excuse himself to the bathroom. When he returned, still chuckling, he said, "You're right. I want you to know that nothing is too much for you. You have no idea what you've given me; you've filled me with so much positive energy and helped me see life through an entirely different lens. Thank you, Anne."

They spent the next few nights together exclusively, and Anne didn't mind. By now, she had realized there was no one else on the cruise who interested her as much as Andy did. They dined together, explored the remaining ports, and spent

time like a couple, though without any romantic gestures, just two very good friends who genuinely enjoyed each other's company. They were constantly talking, laughing, and having a wonderful time, focusing only on the cruise, the next port, and each other.

Last Night Cruising

It was now the final night of the cruise, and they met for cocktails before dinner.

"I have two revelations," Andy said to Anne.

"Really?" she replied, curiously.

"I'll tell you before the night is over," he promised.

She tilted her head and asked, "Andy, what is your real reason for being on this cruise?"

He paused for a moment and then responded, "The truth is, I must retire in a few years, as I mentioned to you during our first lunch together, and I don't have a life I'm happy with. I've worked myself into a mundane existence that I cannot imagine carrying into my third act. I don't want to retire and sit there, decaying. I also fear I'll be in my wife's way when I retire. I don't share this lightly, but I trust you. You hold an incredibly special place in my heart. I'm gathering information so I can put plans in place and make a well-informed decision for the next phase of my life."

Andy continued, "Anne, my life has become very mechanical. I have no fun anymore, and I don't remember

laughing as much as I've laughed this past week with you. I know I need to make some changes. I've been toying with some ideas, but I'm now sure about what I want. I'm grateful we've brought our friendship to this level; I've fallen in love with the life you're living.

I admire the joyfulness of your existence and the happiness I feel being with and around you. I know I can't offer you what you deserve or what you're looking for right now, but I want to ask you for two things: first, I'd like to visit your Caribbean cottage with you, and second, I'd like us to meet on this very cruise again one year from now—if you're free."

Anne looked at him for what felt like an eternity and finally said, "I'm delighted that you admire my life so much. You're welcome to visit my home, and yes, I'll meet you on the cruise—if I'm still free."

Andy smiled warmly and asked, "So, when will you be at your cottage next?"

"In about a month," she answered, then added with a playful smile, "And you'd better mind your manners when you visit."

He grinned and nodded in agreement.

That evening, they danced, sipped cocktails, laughed, and brought the cruise to an exceptional close. As they parted for the night, Andy said, "I still have another confession to share with you."

"Oh yes, that's true," Anne replied, "What is it?"

He hesitated before admitting, "I love being with you. You are incredibly special to me, and I haven't felt this joyful, youthful, and playful in a long time. Thank you, Anne."

As she was leaving him to retire to her room, she turned and said softly, "Everything needs harmony to flourish; two people cannot thrive without it. We have that harmony, and that's why we enjoy each other so much. Each relationship has a 'soul,' and the soul of our relationship is happy and beautiful. That's something I often notice in couples—the 'soul' of their bond. For many, that soul isn't happy."

Andy went to his room, replaying her words in his mind, finding them deeply intriguing. As he settled in, he whispered to himself, "Water now tastes like wine. Everything looks brighter. There's meaning in my existence again, and I want to wake up tomorrow to have breakfast with her one more time before we part."

The next morning, the last day of the cruise, Andy was among the first to stand on the balcony and watch the sunrise. He looked around for Anne, but she wasn't there. She appeared a little later.

"Anne," he said with quiet contentment, "I'm so glad I came on this cruise. It's one of the best decisions I've made in the last decade or so."

She smiled and replied, "Andy, the sum of this week is like an excellent sentence in the paragraph of the chapter in the book of our lives."

He sat in silence, reflecting on her words. After a few moments, she continued, "You can't be happy if your heart isn't in what's before you. You must feel excited and appreciative of life and what it offers. You need to look forward to the opportunities ahead, many of which lie in the simple things you love. When you move in the direction of what you enjoy doing and visit places you love, you stay alive. Without that expectation of the next good thing, life becomes dull and uninteresting."

Andy listened quietly, captivated by Anne's philosophy on life. She went on to describe the simple beauty of blue skies filled with drifting clouds, how she loves lying peacefully beneath them, identifying their ever-changing shapes, something that costs nothing but brings immense joy. Then she looked at Andy and said gently, "You know, we could love each other for the rest of our lives and still love the people who are already in our lives. We can do that. I don't need to take anything away from your family. I would love to be part of your family alongside your wife as the good friend I am.

My position is simple: I've worked hard and suffered much loss, and now I want to live beautifully and enjoy the fruits of my labor while I still can. I don't want my eyes to grow dim from a life of boredom. I'm exploring the things I love—that's what you see in me. Loving life, appreciating what I can do and where I can go. I only do what I love, and I make everything special and meaningful."

Andy thought to himself, *Who is this woman? What an experience this has been.* His thoughts drifted to his marriage.

Over twenty years ago, he decided to marry, and it was the right choice. The world was younger then, and so was he when he committed to his wife, promising to love and cherish each other for the rest of their lives.

I've kept that commitment, he reflected. The truth was, they still loved each other. But now, the world was older, and so were they. They wanted different things. What nourished him in his youth no longer fulfilled him. As the world aged with him, he longed for new warmth and new meaning in his life.

I don't want to live in an 'old, cold' world when there's still warmth to embrace, he thought. *I won't hurt my wife in any decision I make. I'll have to open my heart to her; explain the depths of my soul and the needs I now have… and hope she'll meet me halfway. I'd settle for that. I'd love for her to continue this journey with me.*

Still, the vision of retirement haunted Andy. The thought of being at home with his wife under the current circumstances felt terrifying.

When you have a dream to look forward to and work toward, you're never truly alone, because that dream keeps you alive, and Andy now had that dream. He imagined the life he could create, and because of that, he no longer felt alone. He hoped to enjoy a fulfilling retirement with his wife by his side.

More than anything, he wished he and his wife could share the kind of joy and excitement Anne carried within her. Ideally, he thought about integrating Anne into his life as well and

seeing how his wife felt about her, but he knew that would not work. Andy's heart was full of thoughts, dreams, and possibilities. He wanted to ask his wife meaningful questions and give her time to consider the answers. His greatest hope was to make a decision that honored them both. He hadn't married his wife to leave her; he wanted them to grow together in this third act of life, bringing back some fun and excitement they both deserved.

Home From Cruising

Andy had just experienced one of the best weeks of his life in over a decade. He felt rejuvenated and had a clearer vision of what he wanted moving forward. In a month, he planned to visit Anne at her country home in the Cayman Islands, and he was looking forward to it immensely.

Visiting Anne's Country Cottage

A month after the cruise, while Andy was still sorting through his thoughts, he prepared to visit Anne at her country cottage. He told her, "I am coming for a week, but may change my reservation to two weeks, as I might want to stay in the area and explore a bit. If I like it after my time with you, I'll check into a hotel or guesthouse to continue my exploration."

Anne reassured him, "You are free to stay here as long as you like. If you stay longer than a week and I have to leave, you can remain here without any issue."

"Thank you, Anne," he replied warmly.

Anne arrived at her country cottage a few days before Andy's visit and spent time making sure everything was in order. She had a few people who cared for the property: one maintained the modest but charming grounds; another, an older lady from the village, handled the cleaning; and two others were called as needed for repairs. Anne ensured everything was ready and had the guest room refreshed and tidied up for Andy.

When the day of his arrival came, Anne decided to pick him up herself from the airport so she could give him a tour of the area, which Andy thoroughly enjoyed. He was amazed at the amenities available in the countryside and delighted when they finally arrived at her cottage.

Her cottage sat on a corner lot and had two entrances: one from the main street and another from a side street that led into the backyard. The side entrance was primarily used for gardening deliveries and additional parking during parties. The cottage itself was an old English-style home of modest size, situated on a generously sized property.

In the backyard stood a tiny home, built years ago for house staff. Anne had lovingly furnished it with pieces she adored, creating a cozy retreat. When she spent time in the backyard, she had everything she liked within reach. Though she primarily used the small house herself, she allowed her housekeeper to stay there whenever she wished, especially when Anne was away from the island.

Andy asked curiously, "What shaped you into the person you are today? Have you always been like this?"

Anne paused before answering, then shared that she had essentially raised herself from a young age. Her mother had been very immature, consumed by constant worry over her father, who was a "rolling stone." As her mother was often distracted, Anne had to become independent early on, taking responsibility for herself during her pre-teen years, and even looking out for her mother.

She explained that her vivid imagination developed as a coping mechanism for the neglect she experienced as a child. As an adult, her imagination played a significant role in envisioning the life she desired and the elements that would contribute to achieving it and her happiness. Being independent became her priority. Her childhood taught her never to rely on a man or anyone else for survival. To accomplish that independence, she pursued education and worked hard to secure a stable, well-paying career.

Anne also revealed that her father had numerous extramarital affairs, which made both her and her mother deeply uncomfortable. However, her mother chose to remain in the marriage, perhaps for convenience, financial stability, and to have someone to blame for her unfulfilled life. Anne often felt her mother used the structure of marriage as an excuse to avoid responsibilities, preferring to 'just exist' under its umbrella rather than take charge of her own life.

One of the most cherished gifts Anne received from her father when she was a pre-teen was a fully furnished dollhouse. She adored it, believing it sparked her passion for architecture, interior design, and decorating. She would redecorate the dollhouse repeatedly, gaining immense satisfaction from experimenting with different layouts and styles. That creative outlet fueled her ambition to become an architect and home designer, ultimately leading her to a lucrative career.

Anne admitted that she often felt more like a parent to her mother than a child. After completing her education and moving away, she stayed focused on her goals, building a comfortable and independent life for herself.

At thirty, she fell in love, married, and enjoyed a decade of happiness until her husband decided he wanted out of the marriage. Reflecting on her past, Anne realized that while she should have spent her childhood playing and having fun, she was forced into an adult role far too early. As a result, she now allows herself to indulge in the things she enjoys and never denies herself experiences she missed out on as a child.

Even during her marriage, Anne often felt alone, as though she were never truly part of a union. In her view, the 'real' relationship was between her husband and his mother, while she felt like an outsider. Her husband was overly attached to his mother, who influenced his decisions. Whenever they planned something together, he would consult his mother, who would interject her own preferences, prompting him to change course. After years of this, Anne became increasingly

frustrated and eventually concluded that she would be better off on her own. So, when her husband asked for a divorce, she had no reason to object.

After the divorce, Anne devoted herself to creating the life she desired, a life she could afford, sustain, and enjoy on her own terms, complete with the frills and comforts she loved. She takes nothing for granted and deeply appreciates everything she has. She often says that she is merely a steward of the blessings God has given her and that, when her time with them is over, He will pass them along to someone else who deserves them.

Anne is alone in life, having lost both parents, and she may have some distant relatives, but that's just what they are — distant relatives. She has a handful of very close friends and many acquaintances. And is contented with her life.

Anne's Inspiration For Her Second Home

Anne was born and raised in Connecticut. After completing college, her father gifted her a trip to Barbados as a graduation present. She went on that vacation with two of her close college friends, one of whom had visited several Caribbean islands with her parents and fell in love with the region.

During this trip, Anne and her friends stayed at the vacation home of one of her father's friends. The house, located on a beautiful street, was breathtaking. From the

moment they left the airport, they were captivated by the lush tropics, swaying palm trees, and whitewashed tree trunks lining the roads. The trees were painted with whitewash (*a form of paint used in barns on tree trunks in tropical areas for beauty and protection*) from their roots to about two to three feet up, giving the trees a pristine charm.

When they arrived at the vacation home, they were impressed by its simplicity and beauty. Coming from Connecticut, the climate was a revelation. There was no need for thick sweaters, heavy coats, boots, hats, or gloves; the temperature matched their body temperature perfectly. It was a warm, welcoming environment that seemed to soothe them after their years of college studies and to refresh them for the next leg on their journey.

As Anne settled into her room, she noticed a dozen beautiful summer dresses hanging in the closet. They belonged to the owner's wife, who left her clothes there to use during her visits. Anne was fascinated, realizing this wasn't just a vacation property; it was a true second home. The experience planted a quiet desire in Anne's heart: one day, she wanted a second home of her own. She was not envious of what she saw; she got inspired and saw a way of life that she liked and could work towards someday.

She initially imagined achieving that dream alongside a husband, but she knew, even then, that she wanted it regardless of her marital status and would work hard to make it happen.

The housekeeper at the vacation home told the girls, "Oh, the Misses comes here whenever she likes, sometimes for a week or two, and sometimes for months. Maybe she comes when she and her husband argue, or perhaps she wants her own space to relax and enjoy some selective solitude."

Anne never shared her inspiration with anyone; she kept it locked in her heart as one of her secret wishes for her future. While her friends enjoyed the trip, she carried away a vision —a quiet dream that would eventually shape her life.

Anne Acquires Her Vacation Cottage

Anne's career advanced to the point where she was accepting clients from across the country and internationally, not just from the area around her Connecticut design studio.

She was recommended for a project in Dominica, and the client was so pleased with her work that she received several more referrals. Soon, word about her talent began spreading across other Caribbean islands.

During a vacation to the Cayman Islands with one of her friends, Anne fell in love with the place. She felt that it was somewhere she could one day retire to. As part of her routine, she purchased a local newspaper — something she did wherever she visited — and began by browsing the 'homes for sale' section. She did that because sellers often want someone to improve the property if it's not selling fast enough. But this time, she was looking at homes for sale in a place she fell in love with. Spotting a few homes for sale that caught her

interest, she prompted her friend to go for a drive around in a few areas to do some sightseeing, as she wanted to explore the possibility of doing some work for a client here. She did not feel free to let her friend know precisely what her intention was, as she knew she would be discouraged, and she did not want that. This was a deep desire of hers.

The next day, they visited the area to look around. Anne didn't speak to anyone or make inquiries; she just wanted to see the properties and get a sense of the surroundings.

Although she had long dreamed of owning a second home, Anne wasn't seriously considering it at the time. She was enchanted by the islands and wanted to explore their possibilities, feeling an undeniable calling to the place. To her surprise, one area exceeded her expectations, and the dream of owning a retreat here began to take root as they drove around. Anne didn't need to call any agents or meet anyone, as the information in the newspaper had all she needed to make contact.

They looked at a few properties, but one in particular stood out. It was a cottage close to the beach. The beach was at the back of the cottage within a two-block walk. Anne looked at it thoughtfully, wondering if such a place could someday be hers.

That space of property between the cottage and the beach was full of grape trees, coconut trees, and other fruit trees, along with some unattended tents left there.

That stretch of public property from the cottage to the beach was beautiful, with no buildings, providing a clear view from the cottage.

The cottage included two buildings: a main cottage and a smaller guesthouse at the back, situated on a charming corner lot.

As the vacation continued, Anne kept thinking about the homes and the area. She loved wandering around the islands, soaking in their beauty. Anne was falling in love not just with the scenery, but with the idea of an opportunity she had seen in her mind's eye to have a vacation home. Her vivid imagination, which was nurtured since childhood, especially when she felt neglected, became very active as she pictured herself living part-time on the islands and eventually retiring there full-time.

She could not share her excitement with her friend, who wanted to travel and see the world, which was perfect for her, and Anne supported that. But her friend always wanted to decide what Anne should have and what was enough, and did not genuinely support her. Anne felt there was a low level of jealousy, so she had to pretend she was exploring for a client while keeping her excitement in check and putting all she was seeing in her mind to marinate later.

Anne had prayed to God for guidance, protection, and direction on acquiring this vacation home. She had drawn sketches of what she would like and placed them in her Bible, and left them there for years. The property was not precisely

what Anne sketched, but it shared a few similarities, making it perfect for what she knew she could do with it.

Within a year, and without much effort, Anne managed to acquire the cottage in the Cayman Islands. She was overwhelmed with joy and disbelief at the reality of her long-held, secret dream coming true.

Immediately after the purchase, she traveled back to the islands to spend time at her new cottage, meet her neighbors, and explore the local amenities.

She shared nothing with anyone as she did not want their input. Anne believed in holding her dreams close to her heart until they became a reality – something she learnt the hard way. As people never want you to rise higher than their waistline, some may allow you to reach their shoulder, but never eye-to-eye.

While there, she began planning repairs and how she would decorate the home to suit her tastes. She felt vibrant and alive, almost as though she were floating on a cloud, and had to ground herself amid the excitement; everything aligned perfectly; she met exactly the right people to handle the repairs and ongoing maintenance. Remarkably, those same individuals continue to look after her property to this day.

Revelation At The Cottage

Years after acquiring her cottage, during one of her vacations, Anne lay on her bed one afternoon, glancing at a few dresses hanging outside her closet. She had left them there

after days of indecision about what to wear. As she contemplated putting them away, a sudden realization washed over her: she had silently prayed for an opportunity like this, a second home, fully furnished, filled with things she loved, away from her primary residence. This was her private retreat, her sanctuary. She was living the very dream she had once dared not speak aloud, and she felt deeply grateful and happy.

Life Between Two Homes

Having her second home allowed Anne to feel as though she was always on vacation and always going home; she scheduled her travels around her work and personal life, often heading to the islands whenever she had at least a week between projects. The cottage became nourishment for her soul, especially as she spent more time there during the long, cold months in Connecticut.

When she had first dreamed of such a place, she had imagined sharing it with a husband. But now, as a single woman, she found it equally fulfilling in an entirely different way. The cottage gave her freedom; if she wanted to get away, she could, as she always had people there to do things with and to assist her as needed.

Whenever she visited, she spent her days cooking delicious meals, shopping at the local markets, and mingling with the locals while supporting their small businesses. She loved visiting the piano bars and restaurants in the area, feeling perfectly comfortable going out by herself. Sometimes her

housekeeper, who had also become a close friend, would join her, and a few of her lovely neighbors would spend time with her whenever their schedules allowed.

Anne especially cherished her beautiful backyard, shaded by a magnificent hundred-year-old Tamarind tree. Sitting beneath it helped her feel grounded and connected to herself. For Anne, the cottage wasn't just a vacation home—it was her personal retreat, and every visit felt like a blessing.

Andy At Anne's Cottage

When Andy arrived at Anne's cottage, she welcomed him warmly and immediately showed him to his room. Anne had always valued knowing where she would be staying whenever she traveled, whether it was a hotel, a ship, or a friend's home; it gave her a sense of comfort and belonging.

After helping him settle in, she invited him to meet her in the kitchen for a snack before giving him a tour of the cottage and backyard.

She had prepared a fresh, colorful salad and a platter of fruit, which they shared. Then Anne said, "I need to go to the market. Would you like to come with me?" Andy, delighted by the invitation, readily agreed. Anne grabbed a rolling basket, slung her crossbody bag over her shoulder, smiled at Andy, and said, "Come on, let's go!"

The market was within walking distance, so they strolled there, chatting along the way. Andy felt as though he were

having an out-of-body experience; he had never done anything like this.

The open-air market buzzed with life. Vendors shaded their stalls with colorful fabrics, canvas sheets, or makeshift plastic covers, while some had permanent stands built to secure their produce overnight. Flags fluttered from stall to stall, adding to the lively, festive atmosphere. The energy was infectious.

Many vendors called out cheerfully, announcing what they had for sale that day. It was the kind of place where you could go not just to shop, but to connect with the locals, with the culture, even with yourself. People lingered there for hours, savoring the conversations, the music, and the sense of community.

Anne wanted Andy to experience all of this while also picking up groceries and a few of her favorite treats for the week ahead. She also guided him to some of the boutique stands selling beautiful scarves, jewelry, dresses, blouses, hats, bags, sunglasses, and more. Showing him that even with a modest budget, one could find something special here—and the vibrant atmosphere itself was a priceless part of the experience.

Several of the vendors recognized Anne and called out to greet her; she was happy to see them all. She picked from the fresh produce and encouraged Andy to help choose items he liked, involving him in the process. Andy carried the rolling basket while Anne chatted with the stall owners, and he found himself genuinely enjoying the experience. After about an

hour, they treated themselves to ice cream cones and sat together, soaking in the lively surroundings. Anne noticed Andy's blissful expression. He seemed entirely at ease in her world.

On their way back to the cottage, they passed a wine shop, and Andy suggested stopping to pick up a special bottle for dinner.

That evening, while they relaxed, Andy turned to Anne and said softly, "I love you… And I don't want anything to damage our special friendship. Right now, I love the way things are. We have no complications, and we share an intimacy that's rare and precious. I believe it's more important than sex. Sex can be complicated, and I'm still married, so I don't want to complicate your life. I love and respect you."

She responded, "I am in love with you from the waist up. And I do not believe in adultery, as no one escapes unhurt, and that hurt runs deep. I have a few friends who felt they had to be with certain men because they were in love, but those men were married. They would constantly say, 'I love him.' But I would ask them: if they went to a store and saw an item they could not afford, would they steal it? Mingling with a married man is being covetous, and that is a sin according to the Bible. You are in lust, seeking to please the flesh. It is a terrible thing, especially when you are older and should have gained some wisdom. It is awful!"

Anne's cottage kitchen was very unconventional yet beautiful. It was furnished with old-fashioned kitchen utensils

that still worked perfectly. There were no modern cupboards; instead, open shelves displayed a collection of colorful dishes, mugs, and drinking glasses. The kitchen sink sat beneath a charming old bay window that extended about two feet outward. Inside the bay of the window, various herbs and crystals hung from the top of the windowsill, casting beautiful rays of color that added to the peaceful, playful, vibrant energy surrounding Anne and her cottage.

She shared with Andy that when she acquired the cottage and had some repairs done, she did not want to change anything that would compromise the home's charm.

Anne had plenty of modern technology in her main home in Connecticut. The refrigerator, stove, security system, and lights were all modern and connected to her cell phone. But at her country cottage, she refused to upgrade anything; as long as things worked, she was happy and intended to keep them that way. She even stored a few bottles of wine in her backyard, which she called her 'cellar.' She wrapped the bottles in foil, placed them in holes she dug in the yard herself, and covered them with old, brightly painted square boards. She explained to Andy that, before refrigerators, people stored perishables this way, and she had seen a documentary showing that such methods still worked if you had access to the earth. Andy shook his head and said, "I know." She loved doing these simple, hands-on things.

After they finished their work in the kitchen, Anne took Andy to her backyard. He tried his best to contain his excitement, but after traveling, going to the market, and

helping in the kitchen with an apron on, he finally sat under the 100-year-old Tamarind tree, then said to Anne, "Let me sit here for a while. I have never experienced anything like this."

Anne decided to sit next to him, leaving enough space for him to stretch out without touching her. She said, "If I ever had to choose between the two places I call home, I would choose this one. This place has a soul, and my soul connects with it each time I visit. It always calls me back when I'm at my main home." Andy closed his eyes and remained silent, as did Anne, letting the moment settle between them.

After a while, Andy slowly opened his eyes and asked, "What else do you need in life? Is there anything you are still aspiring to achieve?"

She replied, "Yes, I have things I want to see materialize in five years, some in ten, and others further down the line. In life, you must have dreams; otherwise, you are simply inhaling and exhaling, becoming redundant, and I resent that. I will have a dream until I can no longer dream."

Andy felt as though Anne had been reading his mind; he completely agreed with her philosophy on life. Then she added, "If I don't enjoy my life and make the best of it, who will?"

Andy's thoughts began to wander. If he left his marriage and his wife was comfortable, would she still be cordial toward him? This was important to Andy. Throughout his career, he saw where some people held their significant other hostage after a divorce, and he did not want to have that experience.

Some elderly people say that you are eternally bound to your first wife and God deals with you according to how you treat her. Andy knew he would do well by his wife and wondered if she would give him the freedom to move on and live his life as he wanted.

Despite her mechanical approach to life, he still loved her, finding comfort in the familiarity of what he knew. Yet the fear of the unknown lingered, though it wasn't enough to make him accept and be content with his current situation.

He realized he needed to prepare questions to present to his wife, hoping she would understand his perspective and meet him halfway, or at least find common ground. As he sat with Anne beneath the Tamarind tree, his thoughts turned somber, leaning toward melancholy. Still, he clung to the hope that his wife might be flexible enough to accept some of the changes he craved.

Later, coming in from their time under the Tamarind tree, they prepared dinner and enjoyed a wonderful evening together, savoring the meal they had cooked and a beautiful bottle of wine Andy had purchased during their market trip.

The next day, they walked to the nearby beach, just a short distance from Anne's cottage, and spent hours watching the waves rise and fall. They relaxed, soaking in the serenity of nature, and enjoyed lunch from a beach vendor, along with several glasses of passion fruit and coconut juice. Afterward, they walked back to Anne's cottage for a quiet, restful evening.

That night, they dined at one of Anne's favorite restaurants, followed by a visit to a piano bar for a nightcap and a peaceful walk afterward. At one point, Anne reached for Andy's hand, initiating the gesture. "This is one of the things I miss being able to do," she told him. "Since you're here, I'm going to make use of you."

Over the next several evenings, they cooked dinner together, read aloud to each other, listened to relaxing jazz music, and Anne showed Andy some of her latest design projects. Andy also requested to sit in the dirt each day, as he enjoyed the grounding feeling it gave him.

One afternoon, a neighbor invited Anne to go fishing the next day. Andy was thrilled as he hadn't been fishing since his teenage years, and eagerly welcomed the opportunity. He enjoyed the fishing trip just as much as he enjoyed the company of the group. He didn't want to miss out on anything Anne was doing; he shadowed her closely, embracing her lifestyle and realizing, little by little, he longed for this kind of existence.

Andy found himself doing things he had never imagined. One day, Anne planned to trim her garden plants, tidy the yard, and do some landscaping. She invited Andy to help, and he didn't hesitate to agree. Before starting, she said, "I'm going to the nursery to get a few flowering plants to spruce up the garden beds. Do you want to come?" Andy eagerly joined her.

Once again, he was in awe of how wholesome life could be beyond the confines of a career. He realized he didn't have

a hobby because he didn't allow himself to indulge in one. His entire existence had revolved around understanding and practicing law. Now, his eyes were opening to an entirely different way of living.

They loved each other without entering a sexual relationship. One evening, Andy said to Anne, "Love is not sex. I'm enjoying every moment with you, and there's no sex involved. This is an experience I will never forget, and I want more of this in my life. It is clear why some people, later in life, marry for compatible companionship. I could do that now."

After a delightful week at Anne's cottage, it was time for Andy to face reality and prepare to return home. He wrestled with the decision ahead of him, knowing it might seem selfish, but he felt deeply that this was a matter of life and death for his happiness. He wondered quietly: was it truly selfish to choose life?

That night, as Andy lay in bed, his thoughts circled endlessly around retirement, stagnation, approaching his wife to express his wants while inquiring about hers, and wishing he didn't have to face this emotional crossroads. Yet he knew this experience had been necessary, marking the beginning of the third act of his life.

Before long, Andy awoke to a new day, to leave Anne and return to his beautiful home in upstate New York.

Leaving Anne's Cottage

Andy and Anne had breakfast and continued chatting at the dining table, which was something unusual for him and his wife, and he liked it. After a long while, he got ready to leave. He hugged Anne and said, "I want to hug you for a long time to see if some of your inspiration and lightheartedness will spill over onto me."

Then he asked her, "What are you doing with the rest of your life? What do you want?"

Anne looked at Andy and replied, "There's a lot that I am privately striving for, and it's too long to tell you at this moment. If I do, you may forget anyway; however, it would be a good conversation for another day."

He looked at her and smiled. Then he stretched his arms out, hugged her again, and said, "I have to hold you for as long as possible because being with you, being around you, feels like a fantasy. It's so beautiful, it feels unreal, and I don't want you to disappear."

Andy left Anne's cottage feeling a deep, abiding gladness that was entirely new to him. Anne knew he had enjoyed the week with her, and now he was ready to start putting his life in the direction he wanted. He knew the first thing he needed to do was have a serious conversation with his wife.

One evening after dinner, Andy's wife came over, kissed him on the forehead, and was about to leave. He held her hand

and asked her to take a seat. His tone was serious, so she sat quietly, looking at him intently.

Andy said, "I followed the rules of life as they were taught to me. Early on, I stayed in school, earned good grades, did my best in college and university, got a job, worked hard, got married, and built a decent life for us. I've been a faithful husband to you, and now, after all these years, I feel empty and lost.

There's a lot I've been thinking about very seriously lately, and I have some questions I need your most honest and sincere answers to because I cannot go on like this, especially going into and after retirement. There is nothing here for me but to rehearse the position of death 'with you' day in and day out. I need to know some things from you."

Andy's wife sat quietly, seeming to digest each word he spoke.

Then he said, "I have some questions written out for you. Take your time and respond to them when you're ready. But first, tell me, are you happy with the way you're living your life, the way things are? Are you willing to consider any adjustments to accommodate my needs? Would you ever reconsider coming to bed with me again? Or doing any of the things married people do, like going on vacations together, having fun together, and changing the way things are as we prepare for retirement? And would you be happier without me if you still had everything you now have that fulfills your life?"

Andy's wife sat in shock and dismay. Then, slowly, she asked, "What do you want, Andy? I know we have a routine life, and we were always happy."

Andy responded, "I want more from the life I have here with you. When a man spends the night lying in bed with his wife and engages in pillow talk, a lot is shared, pondered, and resolved. Without that, I feel lost, lonely, and deserted. And in fairness to you, I've made a suggested list of things I'd like you to reconsider."

He handed her a sheet of paper containing his questions:

- *Are you happy with the way your life is for the rest of your life?*
- *What do you see or want for us?*
- *Would you ever have intimate relations with me again, or allow us to lie vulnerable together and see what happens?*
- *Would you be happier without me if you could still have everything you now have that fulfills your life?*
- *What do I mean to you besides being a provider?*
- *What does retirement look like for you?*
- *What do you suggest I do with my needs, those that God designed me with?*
- *What about selling this home and getting two homes: one as our primary residence, and the other a vacation home? I'm willing to stay here if you don't want to sell for another couple of years or so, but I'd like a second home*

somewhere with year-round warm weather. In addition to the Caribbean, I love Italy.

- *I want us to do things together, such as shopping for our vacation home, going to the market, cooking together, starting a garden, and mingling with the locals around the vacation home. Going out, having dinner, walking hand in hand, and being childlike when we want to.*

- *How do you envision retirement for yourself?*

After looking at the list of questions, she read the first few and sat with her mouth slightly open, unsure what to say.

Andy said gently, "I was happy until my last birthday, when the reality of retiring in just a few years hit me like a ton of bricks. I thought about becoming a professor or starting a consulting firm, but that would be a continuation of what we already have."

"What's wrong with what we have?" his wife asked.

Andy replied, "We exist like two siblings. There's no romance, no nightlife, no sleeping together, no traveling together, no fun, no laughter. Life here is just this house and its maintenance. You're in love with this home and all it entails—which is fine—but what about me? Am I just a provider?"

As his wife continued reading the list in silence, Andy finally said, "Is this all there is? Over the last few months, since my birthday, I've come to realize how mundane our lives

have become. After some soul-searching, I've documented the things I'd like to incorporate into our lives in the future. Please review them and get back to me. You don't have to answer today."

Andy's Desires

- *To grow old where it's warm, where palm trees bloom.*
- *To have a second home, a small cottage, or a flat in a warm place.*
- *To reside in a small town or village, perhaps in the Caribbean or a small Italian village, so that if I become disoriented in old age, someone will know me and point me in the right direction.*
- *I've seen the life I'd like to experience going forward.*
- *I want romance.*
- *I want spontaneity.*
- *I want to be in love in my old age.*
- *I shall not sleep alone every night if I have a wife. If I must sleep alone, then let me truly be alone.*

Andy concluded that he was unfulfilled and unwilling to continue life as it was. The alternative would be to have a fling, but he didn't want that or any extramarital relationship. He knew that if he ever went in that direction, it would not be with Anne. He respected and cared for her far too much to cause her pain.

He admired and loved Anne so profoundly that he wouldn't do anything that might jeopardize her happiness. He wanted the best for her and hoped she would continue living the beautiful life she had created for herself. "I will not build a dream with Anne that cannot come true," he decided.

He had seen many men build dreams outside their marriages, only to have those other women keep them emotionally hostage. For instance, when a married man enters into a relationship with another woman, he becomes emotionally tied to her. And if he later meets someone else who fulfills him more, he cannot pursue that relationship because he is now bound to both a wife and a mistress, which results in a life of resentment, guilt, and entrapment.

To Andy, the complications of an extramarital relationship were endless and senseless. They were flesh-based, not God-based. What Andy truly wanted with his wife was love, romance, spontaneity, and the shared joy of building a second home together.

Andy did not mind being alone if he was truly alone, but he resented feeling lonely even when he had a wife. He wanted to go to bed on as many nights as possible, feeling like a child on Christmas Eve, filled with anticipation, wondering what surprises the morning might bring. He resented the predictability of his life, which felt mundane and almost lifeless. The thought of retiring and simply waiting to stop breathing, like so many others, terrified him. Andy did not want to sit around and decay. Even knowing exactly what he

would have for breakfast each morning and at what time bothered him deeply.

He wanted to let his guard down, laugh, and do silly things with a woman he loved. He imagined sitting in the dirt while gardening, getting messy in nature, going fishing, and taking moonlit walks while holding hands. He wanted to sit and watch the full moon rise, to marvel at sunrises and sunsets. He envisioned trips to the plant nursery to explore new varieties of flowers and seeds, relishing the thrill of planting them and watching them grow, even tending to his own vegetable garden. He wanted to dress up for elegant dinners at restaurants where piano or jazz music played softly in the background, perhaps even places where they could dance. Cruises, road trips, and memorable vacations were also on his list.

Andy dreamed of owning a vacation home in a charming town with a beautiful square, somewhere they could walk, shop, dine, mingle with people, and spend quality time together. He pictured sitting on boardwalks, eating ice cream while it melted down his arms and dripped onto his shirt sleeves, and walking in the rain just for the sheer joy of it. Sometimes, he wanted to stand in his backyard and listen to the sound of rainfall. He imagined shopping for vacation gear, including Hawaiian shirts, large beach towels, swim trunks, straw hats, sunglasses, and playful little accessories. More than anything, Andy wanted things to look forward to: activities, adventures, and places to go.

From the time he rekindled his friendship with Anne and upgraded it, he felt she had awakened the dormant parts of him. He was inspired by her and the way she lived. Everything settled well with him, and now he wanted to incorporate as much of that kind of life as possible with his wife.

Andy often asked himself, "What's the point of any of this if it isn't fun anymore? I've done everything I was supposed to. I woke up on time, went to school, received my grades, landed a job, and stayed on track. But now, do I really have to keep following the same path? I've done what was required, so why can't I finally do what I want?"

He had learned so much from Anne, and now he craved a similar experience, a life filled with joy and meaning. Anne once told him, "I like living in two places because I never get tired of anything. Seeing different scenes keeps me alive and inspired." As Andy reconsidered his life, he found himself longing for the freedom and vibrancy Anne enjoyed.

Author Ralph Waldo Emerson said,

"Once the mind is stretched to a certain dimension, it cannot be returned to where it was previously."

Andy understood this deeply. He wanted to come home to surprises now and then and to bring home surprises that would be cherished. For a while, he arranged to have flowers delivered weekly, but even that became routine and joyless. Sometimes, he wanted the simple pleasure of stopping to choose flowers himself, picking what appealed to him in the

moment, even buying roses from a street vendor on a whim. Andy was quietly rebelling against the life he had built.

He also longed to see his wife in a different light, one that was less proper and more playful. He imagined moments of spontaneity: her running around, wrapped in nothing but a towel that might slip away, skinny-dipping together in their backyard pool at night, or wearing provocative swimwear on occasion. However, his wife was conservative to a fault, believing that certain behaviors were inappropriate at her age. He once told her she was wrong to think that way.

"You should never compare yourself to other women," he told her. "Even if you were as old as dirt, if you're in my bedroom wearing lace panties or sexy lingerie, it's perfect for me. There is no competition. If you keep comparing yourself to others, you'll always find someone younger, taller, prettier, or more educated—someone who has things you think would make you better. Don't do that. Embrace yourself for who you are, exactly as you are. You'd be surprised how many people look at you and wish they had what you have. That's life."

There were nights when Andy went to his wife's room, hoping to negotiate intimacy, only to see her fully covered and buttoned up from head to toe. Discouraged, he would return to his own room, abandoning the thought entirely. It felt like too much effort to gain access to her affections. He secretly wished that, just once in a while, she would sleep with the careless abandon of a "street gal," with something left uncovered, tempting him without even trying.

Andy felt he gave his wife everything she asked for and more, yet he was left without what he needed most—the comfort of a woman. To him, that intimacy was heaven on earth, the thing that made a man feel like a king. Instead, Andy felt like a pauper.

Many months later, after the cruise and his visit to Anne's cottage, Andy found himself busier than ever. He was training three junior attorneys, a time-consuming yet rewarding responsibility.

With Thanksgiving just a few months away, he knew he would spend the holiday with his wife, their relatives, and friends at his home.

Preparations were already underway, as Thanksgiving was one of their most significant events of the year. His wife adored the holiday and went all out to entertain her family and friends.

When Thanksgiving finally arrived, it was a crisp and beautiful fall day. The property was blanketed with leaves in brilliant shades of red, brown, and gold. Andy sat by a large window, gazing outside, and wondered what Anne might be doing and how she would enjoy such a scene. He thought to himself, *I'll contact her in a bit,* and turned his attention back to the bustling crowd around him.

Conversations flowed, but they were the same as the previous year and the year before that. The only new and exciting thing in Andy's life was Anne. He felt he had outgrown the mundanity of those around him. No one seemed

to have anything exciting to share. He silently asked himself, 'Is this all there is?'

Eventually, he slipped away from the crowd, retreating to his study. Closing the door, he picked up the phone and called Anne.

"Hi, Anne. Happy Thanksgiving! How are you?"

"I'm fine," she replied warmly.

"I was thinking of you and wanted to say hi. What are you up to?"

"I'm at my vacation cottage," she said. "A few neighbors and I are about to cook a whole fish in the backyard. It's about three feet long. We bought it fresh at the market this morning while it was still alive, so we had the fisherman clean it for us. Two of my neighbors are building an outdoor fire, and a few others we met along the way will join us later. After dinner, we're heading to a piano karaoke bar near the wine shop you and I visited."

"Sounds like you're having a great time," Andy said.

"I really am," she replied. "Honestly, it couldn't be better, well, maybe it could, but it's wonderful here. I'm so delighted to spend the day with such lovely people."

"I'll call you later," he said softly, and they ended the call.

Andy sat in his study for a moment, wishing he were there with Anne, or somewhere warm, somewhere freer. Inwardly, he admitted, *I feel so lonely and out of place here with my wife, her family, and our friends.*

Like Anne, Andy was an only child, but unlike her, he felt trapped in quiet misery. She seemed fulfilled, vibrant, happy, and at peace, living life on her own terms, always having something to look forward to and always free to be spontaneous. He envied that deeply. Still, he played the role of the good husband, carrying himself through the evening as expected. It was, as usual, perfectly "mundane". Soon enough, it would be time to return to work; he just had to endure.

After Thanksgiving

The holiday was over, and the next day Andy headed to the office. It was a partial holiday, so only a small staff was expected, but he preferred being there rather than staying home. It gave his wife space to reorganize the house with her staff after the large gathering. Despite the quiet drive, Andy felt unsettled and restless. Thoughts of Anne crept into his mind, lifting his spirits slightly. He considered calling her but decided to wait until later. Instead, he turned on some music and enjoyed the pleasant one-hour drive to work.

Getting off the elevator at the office, Andy immediately sensed that something was wrong. As he entered the company through the double glass doors, he noticed unusual activity and an uncommon level of chatter for so early in the morning. Walking toward his office, he saw a group of colleagues with solemn expressions.

He asked curiously, "What's the matter?"

One of his associates stepped forward and replied, "Let's go to your office and sit down… Then he said to Andy, Mr. Doole passed away this morning."

Mr. Doole had been one of Andy's closest friends and long-time partners at the firm. Together, they had built the company, Lord & Doole. They built the practice from the ground up. Working side by side on countless projects and cases. They were the two 'fathers' of the company. Mr. Doole was only two years Andy's senior, which made the news even more challenging for Andy to comprehend.

Andy felt as though the world around him had stopped. He lowered his head into his hands, struggling to process the loss.

"Are you okay?" his associate asked gently.

"No," Andy admitted quietly. "I need a minute."

The associate nodded and left to give him space. After sitting in silence for a while, Andy decided to call Anne.

Confiding In Anne

Andy had grown increasingly close to Anne over time and realized he was developing deep feelings for her. As a man, the thought of intimacy crossed his mind, but he was determined not to jeopardize their special friendship.

Anne was warm and comforting, sharing in his grief. As their conversation came to an end, she said softly, "There's that dash between your birthday and your death day, Andy. What you do with that dash is what truly matters. Don't spend it

stressed and miserable—it isn't worth it. This is sad, but I'm grateful your Mr. Doole didn't suffer."

Her words lingered with him long after the call ended.

That day, Andy returned home still consumed by the sudden loss of his partner. He felt as though he were moving through an out-of-body experience. It wasn't until he attended the funeral a week later that the reality of Mr. Doole's passing began to sink in; he was in shock and denial all along.

Two Weeks Before Christmas

One evening, after dinner, Andy's wife handed him her responses to the list he had given her earlier about his desires, plans, hopes, and expectations. Some of her replies were attached separately, while others were written directly on the original document.

Anxious to know her thoughts, Andy straightened himself and began to read:

My Dear Andy,

I am happy living my life just the way it is. My home is my haven, and I am not ready to part with it. I want the rest of my life to continue as it is now. I envision us staying here for retirement, exploring local activities, and continuing to enjoy our life here. We have a perfect life just the way it is.

Having sexual relations is of no interest to me at my age.

You are my husband, and I love you.

Retirement, for me, is simply a continuation of the life we already have, with a few small things added around the house and in the neighborhood. We can even join the country club and learn to play golf if you'd like.

Regarding your personal needs, I would look the other way and wouldn't question anything.

I am not selling this home.

You know I love cold weather. I don't want to move to the Caribbean or Italy.

I think you're going through a midlife crisis, and I cannot uproot or dismantle my life for that.

Response To Andy's Desires

Andy's requests had been simple, but her responses were firm and final:

- *NO.*
- *We can't live in two places at once.*
- *Not moving.*
- *I will turn my face.*
- *We love each other.*

From her answers, Andy realized there was no flexibility and no room for negotiation.

He began to wonder, *Why is my wife permitting me to have an extramarital relationship? Does she already have one?*

Could it be that she's fallen out of love with me and in love with another?

But even as these thoughts flooded his mind, Andy knew he couldn't go down that path. "If I did," he thought, "I wouldn't be giving that person all of me. They'd only get a fraction, because I'd still be married. And what if I wanted to marry or live with this person someday? How could I move forward like that?"

Searching For Answers

The day after receiving his wife's responses, Andy attended a memorial service for Mr. Doole. While there, he found himself studying the faces of the men around him, wondering: *Are they living like old men? Do they still have romance in their lives? Do some of them have girlfriends on the side? How do they find happiness?*

Andy couldn't shake the question of whether he truly was going through a midlife crisis or if something more profound was missing from his life. With Christmas just around the corner, he decided to postpone making any decisions until the New Year.

In the two weeks leading up to Christmas, Andy cycled through a storm of emotions. At times, he felt angry with himself for being a faithful husband all these years, sacrificing his own needs without complaint. At other times, he grew resentful toward his wife for refusing to compromise or show any flexibility.

He imagined, fleetingly, what it might be like to pay for companionship, just one night of passion, no strings attached. But Andy was shy by nature and knew he could never bring himself to do that.

His father's words echoed in his mind. As a young man, Andy had once been told:

"The worst pain a woman can face is her husband's infidelity. It shatters her self-esteem and self-worth and can plunge her into depression and despair. That's why, when someone is murdered, it's often tied to a love triangle—the investigators always look to the spouse first. Infidelity is a deadly poison, Andy. If you decide to marry, don't hurt your wife. If things no longer work, separate amicably. Divorce isn't ideal. God doesn't like it, but He permits it for adultery. Look at the men who chase affair after affair. Are any of them truly happy? Study it for yourself. There's never a graceful ending for a man who lives that way. You cannot hurt your wife and still expect to find peace."

Those words now weighed heavily on him.

A Necessary Decision

This dilemma felt bigger than any legal case Andy had ever handled, and he'd faced some monumental ones. Concentration became almost impossible, yet he knew a decision had to be made.

He realized this was his last chance for love. Even if he didn't enter another relationship, he needed to start living as a

single man because, in reality, that's what he already was. The mockery of their marriage had become unbearable.

It wasn't easy, but Andy knew he needed to plan a new lifestyle for his 'Third Act.' Acts One and Two were behind him, and he couldn't afford to waste what remained.

He requested another discussion with his wife, but she seemed uninterested, having already made her position clear.

When they finally sat down, Andy explained in explicit detail what he needed to move forward. She refused to compromise.

He told her, "Despite your worries about aging, I love you—every wrinkle, every extra pound, every vein you wish you could hide. None of that matters to me. When a man is truly with a woman, when there's romance and connection, he sees only her. When he chooses her, he accepts all of her."

He confessed that had he not gone to law school, he might have become a monk. "I have a pure heart. I never wanted to run from woman to woman. I've only ever wanted one—at least one at a time. I don't like complexity in my personal life; I leave that for my career. And yes, I could have been with many women, but only one at a time. That's my choice. That's who I am."

Finally, Andy proposed a separation. He wanted it to be amicable and hoped they could remain friends. He assured her that he would provide everything she needed and asked her to be honest if she needed anything more during the settlement.

"Anything you need going forward," he said gently, "Will be yours. I love you, but I want a different life. I had hoped we could build a life together, but it seems there's no flexibility on your end. I propose that we separate for a year and then reassess our situation. Since I am the dissatisfied one, I will make sure that, no matter what I do, you will always have your home."

Andy's wife agreed to the separation and was as cold as stone.

Andy was paralyzed by the thought of separating from the life he had always known. The idea of planning for retirement, facing an uncertain future, and confronting his fears weighed heavily on him.

Questions flooded his mind: *Where would I live? When would I leave? How would I start over?* He wanted to go with only his clothes, a few personal belongings, a handful of awards, and his law books. Above all, he wanted his wife to remain comfortable. Andy was, at his core, a decent man.

Now he needed Anne. He knew she would help him find and secure the right place. He needed a furnished apartment for about a year, a quiet space to think, reflect, and gently separate from the life he had known for so long.

It was clear to him that time away from his familiar comforts would be stressful at first, but he believed it would eventually settle into a new rhythm. He hoped that he would grow from the experience and that, in time, so would his wife.

Anne was there for Andy. She helped him find a flat on the other side of town, a place where he could continue his career for the next year and possibly until his retirement. The immediate goal was straightforward: to get him settled somewhere, even if only for a year.

After leaving his home, Andy moved into a hotel before transitioning into his new flat.

After a few months in his new place, it was finally time for the cruise he and Anne had planned following the initial singles' cruise.

Anne lived her life differently from most people around her. Many of her friends had fallen into routines that felt mundane and predictable. Nothing seemed to excite them anymore; life had become a cycle of doing the same thing day after day, without joy or curiosity. To Anne, it felt as though they were waiting for life to happen instead of living it.

This way of thinking was part of why Anne kept her country cottage a secret, even from her best friend. Her friend's logic was simple: *you can't live in two homes at once.* Anne knew that was technically true, but she also knew you could own two homes and live in whichever one you wanted. When the time came for retirement, she would decide which place best suited her lifestyle.

Anne's career took her all over the country and sometimes abroad, so when she visited her cottage, she kept it a secret. If anyone asked, she would say she was traveling for work. She didn't seek anyone's permission or approval to enjoy herself

because she had learned that many people disliked seeing others happy.

After her best friend criticized her for having 'enough' in life already, Anne stopped sharing much with her other friends as well. She kept conversations light, mirrored what others were saying, and rarely revealed her private joys. Deep down, she understood she had to carve out her own happiness, follow what brought her joy, and protect it by keeping it private.

Recently, Anne realized she needed new friends. Her old ones were no longer stimulating; most were content to sit, stagnate, and 'rot,' as she put it. She resented their complacency. Worse still, some drained her energy entirely. Anne believed many of her friends had settled for mediocrity, perhaps imagining they would get another 'rehearsal at life' where they could finally make better choices.

The Second Cruise - One Year Later

Andy was looking forward to the time away. He had promised Anne he would go.

As Andy adjusted to his new flat and way of life, he saw the upcoming cruise as an opportunity to reflect on his future and keep his retirement plans in focus.

Once the cruise set sail, Anne and Andy settled into their separate cabins, each enjoying the experience to the fullest.

On the first night, Andy felt an unexpected wave of emotion. He realized he wasn't loved as a man; he was loved

as a provider. The thought stung, and he felt vulnerable. Yet amid the emotions, he reminded himself that he was still blessed, alive, had choices, and still had time to shape a different life. The recent passing of his career partner, Mr. Doole, had made him even more determined not to waste the years ahead.

During a stop in Paris on the cruise, Andy and Anne wandered into a small boutique, where an older woman sold scarves, jewelry, and other lovely items. Assuming they were a married couple, the woman suggested Andy buy a particular bracelet for his 'wife.'

Anne smiled and corrected her, "We're good friends, but we're not married."

The woman looked at them closely and said, "When two people are together, their souls blend, and your blended souls are beautiful." She then turned to Anne and added, "Next year will be a leap year. That's the only time a woman can propose to a man on that leap day. You should propose to him then."

She went on to explain, "A year and a day is a very special period of time. It takes exactly that long for the human body to decompose after death. Here in France, where cemetery space is scarce, remains are often removed a year and a day after death to make room for others. So, remember, you have some time until the next Leap Day."

They laughed together, and Andy purchased the bracelet for Anne. After thanking the woman, they left the boutique,

walking in silence at first before looking at each other and bursting into laughter.

That evening, Anne carefully cleaned the bracelet, allowing her energy to flow into it, then wore it to dinner.

After dinner, Andy invited her to his suite to relax and enjoy some quiet time.

She agreed but teased him, saying, "Fine, but remember the rules. Mind your manners."

He smiled, took her hand, and escorted her to his suite.

The view from the suite was stunning, with two floor-to-ceiling glass doors opening onto the breathtaking Paris skyline. The ship was docked for the evening, and the city glittered in the distance.

They lounged on the sofa, talking for hours. Their conversations often started in one place and wandered in many directions, rarely reaching conclusions, but that was part of the charm. They enjoyed simply sharing thoughts without needing to resolve everything.

About an hour later, still deep in conversation, Andy said, "Anne, there's a question I wanted to ask you when I was leaving your vacation home."

Anne smiled. "What question?"

He hesitated, then asked, "What made you decide to have a second home as a single woman?"

Anne replied, "Because I'm single, it made perfect sense to me. And, since I don't have a travel partner and I'm a homebody who also loves exploring new places, I chose that path. As you know, I'm a designer, and I love beautiful things. Having a second home allows me to feel like I'm always on vacation. Every time I spend time at my cottage, it feels like an escape, and I can enjoy it entirely on my own terms. Also, it was a dream of mine right after I completed college.

It also gives me something positive to think about, the upkeep, the little details, shopping for things to enhance the home, and even supporting my housekeeper, who's also a friend and looks after the cottage when I'm away. It works well for both of us; I give her meaningful work, and she helps keep my sanctuary in order.

After spending a couple of years trying to plan trips with friends that never happened, only to be canceled for reasons I found unacceptable, I decided to create my own happiness. My cottage is my 'play pen.' Most people don't have a clear vision for their lives. They go with the flow, prioritizing comfort over risk-taking. But having a vision means making decisions, taking risks, and every decision carries the possibility of failure.

Then again, doing nothing also carries risks. Boredom, depression, and hopelessness can set in if you're not careful.

Some people believe that staying in one place forever is stability, but in reality, it can be stagnation. I enjoy having things to look forward to, and I never seem to have time to be

bored. As I mentioned before, I have attended retreats and spent considerable amounts of money to enjoy such experiences, including sitting in the dirt. Many of those retreats included friends, but the implications of hooking up with people, along with the potential delays, meant that some just followed along without being genuinely interested in the activities. Eventually, I realized it was better to focus on carving out a life for myself, creating a space where I could go, do, and be whatever pleased me.

I have always been comfortable being alone, but lately, I've started to feel that having a companion would be nice. My friends no longer fill the space I once reserved for them; phone calls and social media are now sufficient for maintaining those friendships.

People will put you in a box if you let them. They want to decide how much is 'enough' for you, and if they ever discover that you have more than they do, it can become a problem. Everyone desires different things, and ambitions vary greatly. If someone chooses to play it safe and avoid risks, that is their choice, but they should not impose their limitations on someone who strives for more.

When I was preparing to purchase my vacation home, I was so excited and thought my best friend would share in my happiness… but, given our past, I kept it to myself.

At this stage of my life, I find myself drawn to people who are ambitious and financially secure because they encourage and inspire me. I've had enough experiences with people

taking advantage of me, borrowing from me, and even stealing from me. These days, I prefer to surround myself with content and supportive people rather than those who measure my accomplishments or compete against me. I do not compete with anyone for anything.

I'm grateful for what God has blessed me with and for the accomplishments I've made. I admire other people's success and achievements, but never calculate what I can gain from them. That mindset is also why I would never have an affair with another woman's husband. It's covetousness, and it isn't pleasant – it's something ugly that starts in the heart. God warns us against it in His Word because it destroys lives and relationships. Even if the betrayed partner never finds out, damage is done."

"What God has joined together, let no man put asunder."

"Thou shalt not covet; thou shalt not commit adultery."

The consequences of injecting yourself into a marriage are severe. It's a poisonous pleasure, where no one escapes unhurt. Many men excuse their actions by saying, "I did it because I can," and too often, women allow it to happen.

"Andy, we care deeply for each other, but under no circumstances would I allow our relationship to become complicated. They say a man can only go as far as a woman allows him, and that's true. Yet many women convince themselves they're in love, claiming they adore another woman's husband's qualities, his presence, and his charm, and

lose sight of the reality that when they are focusing on what is not theirs, they are actually blocking their own from entering their lives. That is both foolish and dangerous.

"What are your expectations? If you desire something that belongs to someone else and build your life around obtaining it, calling it "love," that is not love at all — it's coveting, confusion, and self-deception. Real love is a conscious decision, made with clarity and integrity. Decisions based solely on physical desire or emotional longing are driven by the flesh and a deceitful heart - not by God.

There is something about men; they will risk everything they've worked for, including their families, reputations, positions in life, and even their names, to pursue inappropriate relationships. They fail to recognize the danger, destruction, and long-term consequences. Yet they don't act alone; some women consent and indulge, and both become entangled in choices that carry lasting pain."

Andy, as my special friend, I urge you to be cautious. Please do not allow your flesh to rule or control you, for it is our greatest enemy on earth. Recently, I found myself in a situation where an old friend, who had been legally separated from his wife for years, asked me out on a date. During our conversation, I expressed my pride in how he had built his life and the comforts he now enjoys. I encouraged him to maintain that stability and even advised him to stop indulging in the illicit relationships he had been involved in.

I told him plainly: "Clean up your life and turn it over to God. All your life, you've followed the desires of the flesh. Now it's time to bring it under submission. This is your moment to seek God."

After hearing me out, he said, "You are truly my friend, and I love you even more for your honesty."

I responded, "Thank you. I care for you deeply and want to see you flourish in every area of your life. If you were divorced, I would have accepted your offer to start a relationship, that's how much I love you."

Andy looked at Anne, nodding as she spoke, and finally said, "I completely understand everything you just said. I admire your thought process."

Although it was a singles cruise, Anne and Andy spent nearly all their time together, except for sleeping in their separate cabins. The trip mirrored their first cruise in many ways, and they both thoroughly enjoyed it.

On the final evening, Andy seemed a bit down. "It's so wonderful here," he said softly, "I wish the cruise could last longer."

Anne smiled and replied, "I understand, but such is life. Don't let that feeling take away from the beautiful night ahead."

He nodded and said, "You always know the right thing to say. So, what are we having for dinner tonight? Let's make it memorable."

That night, they dined, danced, and returned to their cabins, leaving just enough time to pack before disembarking.

After the cruise, Andy returned to his flat and resumed his quiet life. He focused on his work and training young attorneys while adjusting to being alone during his separation from his wife.

As the months passed and the first anniversary of his separation approached, Andy prepared to meet with his wife as they had agreed.

Completion Of Andy's One-Year Separation

They decided to meet at their home. Andy sensed that his wife was comfortable with how things had been, but out of courtesy, he asked how she was doing. She replied, "I'm fine," showing no sign of reconsidering her choices or adjusting her life to accommodate his wishes.

For Andy, that was telling. Deep down, he knew he would rather be alone than stay married and still feel lonely.

After some polite conversation, he asked if she wanted to reconsider her decision or proceed with the divorce. Without hesitation, she answered, "Let's move forward with the divorce."

At that moment, Andy felt all hope fade. He stood, hugged her gently, wished her well, and left.

That night, back in his flat, he sat alone reflecting on everything. He felt unloved and realized his marriage had been over long before, perhaps from the moment they agreed to separate bedrooms. Since then, intimacy had become rare, almost nonexistent. He wondered if he was unlovable or if his wife had fallen in love with someone else.

Overwhelmed, he shed quiet tears. The next day, he called his office, took a few personal days, and allowed himself time to process, though he remained available for urgent matters.

Within two days, Andy drafted a divorce proposal, ensuring that his wife would retain the home she loved and have the necessary provisions to maintain it.

Thinking to himself, he reflected: *"I've always advised my clients to take care of their wives in divorce, to leave the marriage as amicably as possible. There's no need to fight over possessions gained in love and togetherness. If you want to move on, do so, leave the past behind you as cleanly as you can."*

He also remembered his father's advice from years ago: *"Never hurt your wife."* Though this wasn't the kind of pain his father had warned him about, Andy knew that, in its own way, this was still a deep wound.

During this time, he refrained from contacting Anne because she was traveling and he did not want to share this sad part of his story with her. She knew he was separated and did not know what the outcome would be, but now there was no chance of reconciliation between him and his wife.

Andy worked through the divorce papers, a process that took him a few months. He did not place any urgency on it since this was not what he truly wanted, but he worked on it anyway.

Whenever Andy felt sad, he would think about Anne, and that thought alone lifted his spirits. It was even better when he spoke to her. He often said to himself, '*Each time I hear from her, it's like a symphony that penetrates my soul.*'

Being with and communicating with Anne had made his life more beautiful. Andy realized that life needs vitality just as plants need water, and he was in love with the energy and joy Anne brought into his life.

As Andy completed his divorce papers and prepared to present them to his wife, the fall season had settled in, bringing freezing, winter-like temperatures. The cold weather kept him indoors for days at a time. He was feeling low, trying not to depend too much on Anne for emotional support, but that left him unmotivated. He said to himself,

"I don't feel like dancing or singing; everything and everyone is irritating me. The cold is imprisoning me; I feel trapped, not wanting to do anything but stay in bed under the covers. When it's cold, everything becomes harder to do. Your mind freezes just like the temperature, and I feel frozen in place. Getting dressed in layers of clothing, heavy winter boots, and thick socks is not appealing to me; I feel as though I'm paralyzed and

As the weather improved, Andy gathered himself and took the divorce papers to his wife, who was surprisingly happy to sign them. He asked if she wanted to take a few days to review the offer he had made, but she declined and signed immediately, returning the papers to him.

Andy left feeling empty but did his best to maintain his composure.

The next day, he handed the signed documents to one of his attorneys to finalize the process and file them within 30 days.

Thirty Days Later

During this period, Andy kept his communication with Anne brief and infrequent. He did not want to drag her into his personal dilemma and chose to wait until the divorce was finalized before exploring where things might go between them.

The Divorce

Once the divorce was finalized, Andy decided to deliver the completed paperwork to his wife personally. She had fallen out of romantic love with him long ago, but seemed content to continue living together the way things were. Since Andy was the one who was unhappy and had pursued the divorce, he

wanted to handle the situation with as much dignity and sophistication as possible.

He delivered the papers and told his wife that the belongings she had set aside for him would be picked up shortly. He hugged her and left. Surprisingly, he did not feel as sad as he had expected; instead, he felt a sense of release. It felt right, as though he had stepped into a new chapter of his life.

If you want to learn how to swim, you must get into the water.

Now he was finally in the water, learning to swim.

Returning to his flat that evening, Andy did one of the things Anne had previously complained about —something she disliked doing alone: celebrating a personal victory. But this time, it felt right for him. He enjoyed a couple of glasses of champagne, ordered dinner, and let the evening unfold. Before he knew it, the sun had risen on a new day. He prepared himself and went to the office, continuing his work of training young attorneys while staying focused on moving forward.

About a week later, Anne called to check on him. She had just returned from traveling and was planning to spend two full weeks at her cottage. Excited to catch up, she was making calls she had missed over the past several weeks, and Andy was at the top of her list. Hearing from Anne was like music to his ears. He was now a single man with no strings attached, just like her.

Being in cold New York was not appealing to Andy, especially after hearing about Anne's whereabouts in the

islands, but he had professional commitments that kept him grounded.

This was the first time they had spoken since Andy's divorce had been finalized. Anne asked how he felt, and he calmly replied, "I feel a sense of peace and release from what was no longer working for me. Now, I look forward to designing the life I want for my 'Third Act.'"

They spoke about the weather. Anne said, "I like being in Connecticut in the fall and winter, but not so much in January and February. The thing about this area, though, is that it's good for my business, and I enjoy the expected socializing, the ease of getting to many of my clients, and the proximity to the airport."

Andy replied, "I understand. Now that I'm a free man, I don't feel any excitement about being in New York anymore. Maybe it holds too many memories I want to get away from… so I'm thinking of doing some Caribbean travel to check out a few more places, but nothing too far from your country home."

Andy could hear Anne smiling on the other end of the line. She asked how many Caribbean destinations he had visited, and he said, "About a handful during my college years and a few more during my adult work life." She then asked if there were any he was particularly interested in revisiting.

He replied, "I'd like to go back to the Bahamas and the Cayman Islands… and also explore a few other islands over the next two years to see which one calls to my soul."

Anne asked, "Do you like the Cayman Islands?"

He said without hesitation, "I love it!"

Andy's call with Anne was rejuvenating. He felt refreshed; she was like a breath of fresh air. For the rest of the call, they made plans for travelling to the Caribbean one day, then closed the call feeling fully content.

Pursuit of Passion

In the days that followed, Andy continued dedicating himself to training the young attorneys and discovered a newfound sense of joy. He realized this happiness came from having no expectations of anyone. He was alone by choice, having come to accept that he had to depend on God and himself for whatever he wanted. This realization brought him a deep sense of peace, happiness, and contentment.

In the evenings, after dinner, he spent his free time delighting in his freedom. He found himself craving a slower, more grounded lifestyle, one where he could cultivate a garden, come home early in the afternoons, and spend time nurturing it. Unfortunately, that wasn't thinkable in New York in the flat he occupied, and it would only be possible in the spring and summer.

One afternoon during his lunch break, he visited a nursery and floral shop, where he met an older woman named Milly. She was in her late eighties but moved with the energy and vitality of someone twenty years younger. Andy was immediately impressed by her vast knowledge of plants and gardening.

He told her he wanted to invest in a few plants for his flat. He confessed that he had never had a garden before, as he lived in an apartment with no outdoor space. Milly asked about the direction his windows faced to better understand the light exposure.

Two days later, Andy went home with six plants of various sizes and felt an unexpected sense of responsibility and joy in caring for them.

Andy was adjusting peacefully to his new life and looking forward to retirement, wishing it would come sooner so he could start exploring the many things he had recently developed an interest in. He began researching aquariums and discovered he had the perfect space in his flat to accommodate a 20-gallon tank. Excited, he dove into learning about styles, equipment, and care, which eventually led him to visit an aquatic shop not far from the nursery where he had first met Milly.

Andy became busy with these newfound interests. One day, as he was leaving the aquatic shop, he saw Milly standing in front of the nursery and stopped to say hello. She greeted him warmly, asking how he was and how his plants were doing. Andy, filled with joy, told her about the beauty of his plants and his new hobbies, admitting he couldn't understand why he had never explored them before.

Milly then asked if he had a few minutes for a cup of coffee, and he agreed. They walked to a nearby coffee shop, placed their orders, and Andy insisted, "This one's on me." Milly accepted, and they sat down at a small table for two.

Andy introduced himself, though he already knew her name from the badge on her apron.

Curious, Milly asked, "What inspired you to take up these new hobbies. Are you perhaps trying to fill the void left by a loss?" Andy nodded and said softly, "Yes, I've had a loss recently that created a void in my life."

"I understand," Milly replied gently, then added, "Life has stages, and at different times we need different things." She asked if she could share a story, and Andy encouraged her to go on.

Milly began, "A woman I know worked hard all her life, saving as much as she could for retirement, was introduced to a law firm that specialized in wealth planning. They did a good job overall, but every time she wanted to use some of her money, they'd present her with scenarios explaining why she shouldn't.

On her 80th birthday, she found herself thinking about a dream she had had since her youth and felt she needed to pursue it —because if not now, when? She spent months researching and gathering all the necessary information. On her birthday, she visited the law firm to request a specific portion of her savings. Again, they gave her the same song-and-dance routine, telling her why she shouldn't.

Finally, she said, 'If you don't release my money, I'll close my account and withdraw everything, because what I want to do must be done.' After some back-and-forth, she won and went straight to sign a lease for a floral shop. She had already prepared her supplies, had two staff members on standby, and had everything lined up to launch her dream.

That was seven years ago. Today, that woman, who was then making her way in retirement, not only achieved her dream but grew it. She now owns a successful floral shop, has opened a nursery, employed half a dozen staff members, and collaborates with several suppliers who enjoy working with her."

Andy smiled and said, "Wow! That's wonderful!"

Milly looked at him, paused, and said softly, "I am that 87-year-old lady."

There was a moment of silence before she continued, "Andy, whatever you want to do, do it. Research, prepare, and then execute. I can be your mom. Take this advice: When you have something in your heart that brings you joy, don't share it too soon. Move toward your dreams quietly, and only share them after you've acted on them. You may have one or two trusted people to confide in, but guard the joy of your heart. Not everyone wants to see you happy. Be joyful in silence, work on your plans, and share them later.

When I started my shop, nearly everyone, including my friends and family, discouraged me. But at 80, I had learned enough to stop seeking anyone's advice. They found out only after I had done it."

Andy was in awe. Her story felt like confirmation that his private, introspective way of living had always been right for him. He had spent his life keeping things to himself, even with his wife, and now, as he began charting a new direction, Milly's advice felt like a guiding light.

He thanked her warmly and said, "I feel like I've just made a new friend. I admire you, Milly, and I'll be visiting you

often." Smiling, he added, "And by the way, you don't look your age, you look at least twenty years younger." Then, gently holding her elbow, he walked her back to her shop.

To The Bahamas

Back at his office, Andy couldn't stop thinking about Milly and her story. He felt that there was a reason he had met her, and he deeply appreciated the wisdom she shared. That afternoon, he began wondering what his next step should be and how best to plan his actions.

He decided to start by booking a trip to the Bahamas, a place he had always loved and wanted to revisit. He debated telling Anne, but ultimately decided he wanted to experience it on his own terms. He thought he'd book a short trip and call her once he was already there. For the first time, he wanted to start living fully as a single man, because that was what he was now.

Anne, meanwhile, was busy with her own travels and work, so Andy went ahead and made a week-long reservation. He liked the idea of escaping the cold for a while and enjoying the warmth of the Bahamas, a place full of good memories and beauty.

Two weeks later, Andy arrived in the Bahamas. He checked into his hotel at night, pleased to find his room overlooked the beach just as he'd requested. Though he had some initial fears about traveling alone, he was doing fine. That night, he ordered room service and ate facing the ocean, enjoying the sound of the waves.

The next morning, he woke early and went for a long walk along the beach. On his way back, he explored the breakfast options, which looked appealing. Dressed in swimwear and flip-flops and carrying a large towel, he sat by the beach, enjoying a relaxing breakfast and savoring the sense of freedom.

Andy felt free like a child discovering life for the first time – without parents. It was as though he had escaped a suffocating situation. He couldn't understand why his wife had never been willing to make small changes to improve their lives together, but that chapter was over now. He was embracing his newfound independence.

He realized he had never truly liked winters but had endured them simply because that was the life he had known. Born and raised in New York, he went to school there, built his career, got married, and established his home. But now, the world was opening up to him, and he dreamed of spending as much time as possible in warm, sunny places.

During his years as an attorney, Andy had traveled to Italy many times and had always loved it. He decided it would be one of his subsequent trips as a free man and maybe, just maybe, Anne would like to join him.

To Italy

A few months after returning from the Bahamas, Andy began researching different parts of Italy for a vacation, focusing on regions he had visited before. He decided to mention the idea to Anne.

She was elated and asked, "When are you planning to go?"

He replied, "I don't have an exact time yet, but I'd like you to come with me."

There was a gasp, followed by silence on the line. After a moment, Andy said, "Hello?"

"I'm here," Anne replied softly.

"What happened?" he asked.

She smiled through the phone and said, "Italy is on my vision board for this year, and yes, I'll go with you."

Months later, after finalizing all the plans, they flew to Italy together. Andy booked a beautiful suite overlooking a lively town square, just a ten-minute walk from a popular beach. The suite was spacious enough to provide them with privacy from each other when needed.

They spent eight peaceful and pleasant days there, each day better than the one before.

One evening, Anne told Andy, "I'm happily exhausted. I love being here, with its warmth, people, food, shopping, and proximity to so many other European countries. It's everything and more than I ever imagined from what I saw on cruises. I absolutely love this!"

Andy adored her enthusiasm.

"I wish I had shown you my vision board when you visited my cottage," she said one afternoon.

"Why?" Andy asked, curious.

"Because Italy has always been on it," she explained. "It's one of the places I've dreamed of retiring to. When the time comes, I plan to give up my Connecticut home and exchange

it for a flat in Italy, splitting my time between there and the Cayman Islands."

They were sitting on the sidewalk outside a café when this conversation took place. Andy got up and hugged Anne from behind as she sat in her chair and said, "You are the lady of my dreams. I love your spontaneity and your desire to explore." He added softly, "I love it here." Then he sat back down and began feeding her the rest of the food on her plate.

From the sidewalk, they set off on a spontaneous, carefree day with no particular plan, just going wherever they felt like and wherever transportation was readily available. At one corner, a bus pulled up, and they decided to hop on without even checking its destination. They looked around and enjoyed the scenery as the bus carried them along. They delighted in each other's company, behaving like a couple who had been together for years.

At this point, they were about four months away from the "leap year date," but neither of them was thinking about it. That evening, as they relaxed in their suite, Andy asked Anne whether she would ever consider marrying again or if she just wanted a travel partner. She replied, "Do I have to give you that answer now? Because I'm not sure."

"Take your time," he said gently.

She paused, then asked, "Would you marry again?"

"Yes," he said without hesitation, "to you. But let's not rush anything. I'm still in a vulnerable place and would like to wait a bit. But the answer is Yes."

Andy and Anne both loved Italy and decided they wanted to explore it further.

On the last day of the trip, Andy received a surprise from Anne. He found a love letter from her in his bag when he unpacked. He opened it eagerly and sat down.

Dearest Andy,

My life has been unconventional. I was a very unattractive child, and the adults around me were not shy about letting me know. As I grew older, I found a few friends, but I also attracted people who constantly criticized me — my looks, my body shape, my unruly hair, and more.

Deep inside, however, I always knew that my self-worth wasn't tied to my appearance. So, for the most part, I distanced myself from those people and became a loner by choice. It never made sense to criticize what God created. I didn't create myself, and I was content in my mind, spirit, and body.

There has never been a baby born into this world who compares body parts with other babies. They live happily as long as their diapers are changed and they are fed.

People learn about body types, shapes, hair, and everything that makes up a human, but it seems that only our Almighty Father looks at and values the heart.

At some point, though, I realized that even when surrounded by people, I often felt incredibly lonely. I never had anyone to talk to, so I spent hours playing with my dolls and the beautiful dollhouse my dad gave me — a gift I still cherish to this day.

It also became clear to me that most people take life far too seriously, treating every event as a major crisis rather than seeking solutions. I once read that,

"We don't stop playing because we grow old; we grow old because we stop playing." – unknown.

Today, most of my friends — the few I have — have stopped playing.

Our conversations seem to revolve around the same topics: body shapes, fashion trends, and other superficial subjects that don't really interest me. I've always been drawn to different aspects of life, which has led me to keep more to myself and communicate with others less and less. I find that my own company is the most fulfilling, as it allows me to do what I want, when I want, and how I want.

I watched my mom get sidelined by my dad, who never truly saw her worth. He didn't know what he was searching for, and as a result, he never settled into life with her. That left me to raise my 'unattractive' self in many ways, emotionally speaking.

From a very young age, I knew what I wanted and what I wouldn't tolerate. People often labeled me 'unattractive' and 'difficult,' but neither was true. I had boundaries and wouldn't allow anyone to cross them, which was uncommon among my peers.

I've always had a natural gift for making things better. It was instinctive for me to look at something and see how to improve it. That passion led me to decorating, so I went to school for it, built a successful career, and lived life the way I wanted. I eventually married, spending a decade in that

relationship before finding myself single again — and I was perfectly fine with that. The divorce didn't derail me; it strengthened my focus on myself and my happiness.

Now, I'm where I want to be. I love my work, my travels, and the freedom of having two homes — without anyone waking up one day deciding to fight, disappear, cheat, or lie. In many ways, I've created for myself the safe, peaceful world I didn't have as a child.

As we advance, I've been toying with the idea of having a companion, someone to accompany me to different functions, travel with, spend vacations together, and share time with. Someone I can cook and shop for, hold hands with, and lean on when I need comfort and, just as importantly, someone to celebrate victories with when they come.

For so long, I've celebrated accomplishments alone because it's often hard to share genuine joy with people. Too frequently, they compare your situation to theirs or to someone they know, or they downplay your success altogether. I don't need that kind of discouragement; I've had enough of it. That's one reason I went on the singles cruise.

Online dating doesn't appeal to me; it's a good idea in theory, but I'm old school. However, I've promised myself this: if I don't find a companion within the next year or so, I'll get a puppy.

When I retire, I plan to sell my primary home and live in the vacation cottage. In place of the main house in Connecticut, I will look into a small place in Italy. I'll use that time and freedom to travel to different places where I have friends and acquaintances, spending a month or so in each.

You won't find me staying in anyone else's home during these trips — I love my privacy and the freedom to come and go as I please, seeing who I want and doing what I want.

Once retired, I also plan to work as a consultant in my field, sharing my expertise and mentoring younger, up-and-coming designers. And I'll become more involved in my vacation community.

Life, for me, has reached a point where I am overflowing with love, joy, and peace, and I won't risk losing that by making foolish changes. I treasure our friendship and the intimacy it offers, but I won't take it any further than that. I respect you and your situation, and I have no intention of complicating it.

After reflecting on the lives of those around me — watching how my mother focused entirely on my father and observing friends' choices over the years — I made a decision: I will choose happiness. I've decided to make the most of each day. And on the days when I can't find my joy, I remain quiet and turn inward.

With my dollhouse, I discovered an interest in interior decorating, and to this day, that passion continues to bring me happiness.

I know I've grown into my own now, I've become a swan, and I see that many of those who seemed to 'have it all' when we were younger no longer do…

- *Hair loss*
- *Weight gain*
- *Bad knees*
- *Eye issues*

These days, most conversations revolve around doctors' appointments, medications, and surgical procedures. I understand this is part of life and that I'm not exempt from it, but I refuse to make it my sole focus. The things I didn't have as a young girl and young woman have blossomed for me now, and for that, I give all thanks to my Almighty Father.

Now you have this as a clear outline of who I am and why I am the way I am.

Anne

***

Andy felt a sense of calm after reading the letter. Anne had poured her heart out to him, sharing everything he needed to know. This letter had just helped him make the decision he had been thinking of for some time.

The Leap Year Date

About two months after the trip, Andy had a lightbulb moment about the upcoming "Leap Year Day." He decided to spend the entire week with Anne. He didn't yet know where or how, but he wanted to ensure they were together so she could follow through on the tradition and propose to him.

They continued their lives as best friends, marked by occasional light flirting. They didn't rush into anything. Anne visited Andy a few times at his flat, offering decorating ideas and bossing him around, something he secretly enjoyed. One

day, Andy presented the opportunity of a week-long cruise during Leap Day week.

"That's wonderful," she said warmly. "I think we'll have a great time."

This was Andy's second Christmas since his separation and divorce, and he was adjusting well. The first one had been tough, but now he felt as though the chains were finally falling off.

By the end of February, the 'leap year date,' they were on the cruise. That morning, Anne, who had an inkling of what was coming, woke up as if fully prepared for what was to come. While enjoying the cruise, Anne opened up to Andy in a way that explained what she wanted from Andy and from life.

"Andy, there are times when I want to celebrate an accomplishment… Times when I want to go somewhere new, maybe on a spontaneous trip, which is a last-minute deal to a place I've always wanted to visit, but there's no one to go with me. When I invite friends, they often take a long time deciding. They have doctor's appointments, need to ask their husbands, don't have the finances at the moment, or simply aren't feeling well, and while I understand, I want better for myself.

"The life I'm living now, Andy, is my compromise for not having a significant other. I don't regret my divorce; I believe people shouldn't stay together solely for property or for the children, especially once the children are grown. We all deserve happiness and the freedom to live our lives to the fullest.

"I rarely stay away from my cottage for more than a month to six weeks at a time. Still, there are moments when I want to go elsewhere, and although I do love to travel, visiting certain places alone isn't always appealing. That's why I'm thankful for my cottage, the neighbors there, and the amenities that make it feel like home.

"Living this way has contributed tremendously to my happiness. It continues to nourish my soul because I live intentionally, in ways that bring me joy. I don't wait for anyone else to do that for me. But now, I feel the need to share my life with someone —a partner to experience things with, someone who walks the same path, or at least wants to be on it.

"I want to love someone. I've decided I want to share affection and all the beautiful aspects of life with someone I feel comfortable with—someone who lets me be myself, who doesn't expect me to be serious and 'adulting' all the time, because I often like to embrace my childlike side. And yes, I want passion too, I want to 'roll in the hay.'

"We're given the privilege to enjoy and manage certain things in life, but ultimately, nothing truly belongs to us. We can't take anything with us when we leave this world. And because nothing belongs to us, we cannot truly lose anything either. Life is about gaining, learning, and evolving.

"Too many people are afraid to live, to take risks, to explore, to truly enjoy themselves. I was told long ago that the wisdom we need for each day arrives with each new day, and within that wisdom comes understanding, the knowledge of what to do and how to do it.

"You find meaning in life only when you create it… or when you take the time to discover it for yourself. But don't get trapped in fantasies that turn into nightmares. If you're not actively seeking something, you may not recognize it when it's right in front of you.

"We all need a purpose, a why, a reason to keep moving forward.

"When I retire, I want to spend six months on a world cruise, soaking in new experiences. I want to spend two months in Italy. Looking for a place to invest there.

"To me, retirement doesn't mean stopping work; it means working on my terms. It's about taking on fewer assignments, avoiding unnecessary travel, and focusing on what brings me peace and fulfillment, not simply doing nothing."

Andy, who was silent and let Anne speak and let out all she had been holding inside for a long time, now embraced Anne solemnly. He had now understood that Anne was the soulmate he had always been looking for. Everything she had said resonated deeply with him.

That night, on February 28th, as the clock struck midnight, Anne waited for about five minutes into the next day—the Leap Year Day—and proposed to Andy, just as the old lady had hinted, and Andy accepted her proposal with an excited, "Yes!"

***

Anne shared that she was feeling weary of people who remain drawn to doing the same things in their later adult years as they did in their early life.

She said, "Recently, I have been asking myself and those close to me if they are genuinely enjoying their lives. Everyone hesitated before answering. A few said "Yes," but most admitted they would need to change certain things—or even certain people—before they could be happy. I've noticed that many people are unhappy because they're stuck in situations shaped by decisions made in their youth. They are still living with choices that no longer serve them today. Some people grow up and outgrow what once was, while others remain who they always were with no growth.

Couples, for example, do not always grow together harmoniously; often, they grow apart, wanting different things in life. Yet they remain trapped by past decisions, even when those choices contradict what they need now.

Another thing I must emphasize is that you can never get the correct result by consciously making the wrong decision. Imagine this: a married man chooses to remain faithful to his girlfriend while being unfaithful to his wife, believing he is making a good decision. Where could such a situation possibly lead?

And if, at this point, you are blessed to be in your Third Act of life—sixty years and beyond—I hope you are living a celebrated life, a life filled with expectancy, purpose, and meaning.

I have noticed a troubling pattern among people transitioning from Act Two into Act Three without planning, and making the necessary adjustments burdensome. The truth

is, you must adjust—whether you want to or not, and have a plan for the different stages of life.

At sixty and beyond, if you possess a particular skill and choose to continue your career, that is admirable. However, you must also acknowledge that life is gradually winding down, and at some point, you need to modify your approach. You cannot maintain the same demanding schedule or pace that you kept in your thirties—that was thirty years ago. **Have a plan—or make one now.**

In each act, we find ourselves in a different phase of life and personal development. What we need in Act Three differs significantly from what we needed in Act One or Two. Yet many people attempt to live one act with the resources or mindset of another. For example, you cannot thrive in Act Three using Act One resources.

Thriving In The Third Act

Anne and Andy decided to wait before getting married — possibly until Andy retired — but they agreed to officially start dating and take their friendship to the next level.

When they returned to New York, Andy surprised Anne with a beautiful diamond ring, which she promised to wear forever.

Anne decided that when Andy retires, she'll follow him and retire about a year later. Since she already owns a home in the Caribbean, they plan to purchase a house together in Italy, allowing them to split their time between the two locations.

That night, Andy lay in bed reflecting on his life and how beautifully it had transformed. He now had someone he deeply loved and a vision of fulfilling his 'third act' in retirement. He emerged from the daunting retirement that lay ahead and into this amazing adventure that was now his life.

He felt excited about house-hunting in Italy with Anne and enjoying their Caribbean home together.

When Andy first started thinking about retirement, he was overwhelmed by negativity, convinced that life was at a dead end. He feared retiring only to 'sit and rot.' However, his outlook had changed entirely now. The thought of building a new life with Anne filled him with joy. He looked forward to creating a home with her in Italy.

The only thing he felt was missing was getting Anne a puppy. Smiling to himself, he thought, 'Anne wanted someone to share life and its special moments – and if that did not work out, she would get a puppy.' So, now Andy was searching for a puppy for her because he agreed she deserved one in addition to him—they both had enough love to give, and would enjoy having a puppy to care for. She worked hard and faced many of life's challenges alone, so he wanted her to have him and a puppy…

Andy told Anne, "Since I'll handle all the finances for the home in Italy, you're free to start planning your retirement and selling your home in Connecticut. We'll join our strengths and resources and walk in the same direction."

There's an old saying: *'Two can't walk together unless they agree.'*

And Anne and did agree. What an incredible turn of events had taken place in Andy's life, one he had silently prayed for - and God Almighty had given him. Here he was, finally, living his last chance for love.

The End